Latchkey Girl

Heartlines

Heartlines

Pam Lyons

Latchkey Girl

A Pan Original

First published 1983 by Pan Books Ltd,
Cavaye Place, London SW10 9PG
9 8 7 6 5 4 3 2
Pam Lyons 1983
ISBN 0 330 28201 8
Phototypeset by Input Typesetting Ltd, London SW19 8DR
Printed and bound in Great Britain by
Hunt Barndard Printing Ltd, Aylesbury, Bucks

Chapter 1

'Hi! I'm home!' I kicked the front door shut with the heel of my foot and plonked my school bag on the polished mahogany hall chair. 'Mum! Where are you?' I called up the stairs as I made my way through to the kitchen. But the house was silent. I stood for a second waiting, listening for a sound – any sound – to indicate that I wasn't in the house on my own again. But all I heard was the ticking of the grand-father clock from the open-plan sitting room and the buzzing of the refrigerator.

Mentally, I checked that it was Wednesday. 'Of course it is, stupid!' I told myself aloud, breaking the echoing silence of the still house. And on Wednes-days, Mum was always home. But not today, it seems, I corrected myself as I opened the fridge door and peered inside to see what I could find to drink. I pulled out a bottle of lemonade and a piece of pork pie then, placing them on the Formica-topped table, went in search of a glass. I found one on the draining-board and was just pouring the sparkling, fizzy drink into it when the phone started to ring. Still holding my drink and biting a large chunk out of the pie, I walked back down the passage to the hall to answer it, guessing it was Mum.

I was right.

'Where are you?' I demanded between mouthfuls of succulent pork.

'I'm still at the store, pet,' she said, sounding flustered. 'I tried to ring earlier but there was no reply.'

I swallowed the last piece of crust and mumbled that I'd been delayed. I didn't bother to explain that I'd actually had another detention. After all, she never bothered to question me on my time-keeping. 'Why are you still working?' I asked. 'Wednesdays are your half-days. I thought we were going to the cinema this evening?'

'I know, pet, but something's come up. Look, I can't explain right now because I've got to go into an important meeting, but I'll tell you later. It's very exciting.'

I felt a sinking sensation in my stomach as I realized that she'd avoided answering my question about seeing the film. And even without asking I knew what she expected me to do. It was the usual pattern.

'How about jumping on a bus, Ronnie and going over to see your Gran? I've already had a word with her and she'll have something ready for you to eat. I'll pick you up from there, later, when I've finished here. Now, I must rush. They're waiting for me. 'Bye for now.'

' 'Bye,' I replied, tonelessly, and let the receiver fall back on to its cradle. I stood staring at it for a second, gently kicking the hall table with my toe. Then I turned and stomped back to the kitchen to refill my glass, feeling both angry and disappointed. That was the second time Mum had let me down about seeing the film at the Classic. It was a reshowing of *Raiders of the Lost Ark* and I'd wanted to see it for ages.

Well, there were only three more days before it was taken off, so Mum had better make arrangements to see it before then or ... or ... Or what? I asked myself feeling suddenly tearful. What are you going to do? Shout? Scream? Have the sulks? It wouldn't make any difference, I knew that. Mum had a marvellous knack of diverting a head-on collision and what started out as the beginning of an argument always petered out when she started making fun of my moods.

I sighed and glanced at the kitchen clock. If I hurried, I'd catch the five o'clock bus. And if I really hurried I could do a quick-change out of my school 'blues' and sling on my jeans and tee-shirt.

'Where to?' the driver asked as I got on the pay-drive bus.

'Scudmore Road,' I told him, handing over twenty pence.

The driver slid the change into the money compartment and rolled out a ticket for me. 'There's plenty of room upstairs,' he informed me without looking up.

I grabbed the ticket and sauntered through to the already crowded lower deck. Scudmore Road was only two stops and I had no intention of climbing up the narrow, awkward stairs to please anyone!

'Hey! That was my toe, miss!'

I glanced across at an irate-looking, middle-aged woman who was sprawled over two seats, her overflowing shopping bags on either side of her. 'So-*rry*!' I said in a sing-song voice, and she gave me a nasty look. I stood my ground and stared pointedly at her bags. 'Do you mind very much if I sit down?' I said, smiling sarcastically at her. 'After all,' I added, 'these seats were designed for *two* passengers, you know.'

I watched with an amused expression on my face as the woman tried to gather a bag on to her ample lap and shift her weight across towards the window. It was a losing battle! I made a great fuss about sitting squarely on my side of the seat. 'Thank you,' I said, still smiling sarcastically at her.

Her heavy cheeks grew pink with rage. 'Kids!' she hissed sideways at me. 'No respect!'

I pretended not to hear and gazed round at the other passengers. There were a couple of sixth form girls from Parkhill Comprehensive, and one of the boy prefects. By the looks on their faces I could tell they'd overhead, and seen, everything. So what? I thought. Who the heck are they, anyway? I'm not in school now. I gave them all one of my superior smiles and turned my attention back to the woman beside me. 'I'm getting off at the next stop,' I said, falsely polite. 'So you may spread yourself out again, okay?'

I stood up, ran down to the exit doors and rang the bell three times once I had got there, aware of the mutterings of the woman from behind me and the angry glance from the driver at my insistent ringing. The doors swung open and I jumped out on to the pavement, and almost fell on to a boy who was waiting at the bus stop. 'Hey! Watch out!' I cried, trying to avoid him. He side-stepped – but was too slow and our bodies collided.

I felt a pair of strong hands trying to steady me and then I also became painfully aware that the boy was standing on my foot. He was tall – and heavy!

And obviously totally unaware of my toes under his sneakers!

'You're on my foot!' I yelped, pushing away from him. I glanced up, ready to give him a mouthful – but stopped short. A pair of dark, chocolate-brown eyes were gazing kindly into mine.

'I'm sorry. Really,' he said. Then, as we heard the bus doors begin to swoosh close, he shrugged helplessly and made a deft leap on to the platform.

I stood rubbing my bruised foot as the double-decker pulled away. The boy with the brown eyes was still looking back at me, through the window. He was smiling a funny, sort of lop-sided smile and, despite my bruised foot – not to mention, pride – I couldn't stop myself from smiling back.

Scudmore Road is lined with poplar trees and the semi-detached houses are set back from the pavements, fronted by long, neatly-laid out gardens.

Number sixty-eight, number seventy, I said to myself as I trailed along towards Gran's house. Seventy-two ... a cat shot out across my path, and I stopped, recognizing the unusual, silver-grey fur and long, bushy tail. 'Here, Merlin!' I called, crouching down and twiddling my fingers for Gran's cat to come to me. Merlin stood arching his back, his tail twitching in the late afternoon sunshine, his peculiar yellow eyes watching me with a curious, detached look in them. 'Come on, fat cat!' I called. 'It's me, Ronnie.' I reached my hand towards him and he poked his snub nose forward to smell my fingers. I leaned a fraction closer and caught hold of him, then lifted his heavy, furry warmth against my shoulder. He snuggled close and I buried my face into his musty-smelling coat and nuzzled him as he began to purr contentedly. And, still cuddling him, I walked the last few yards to number seventy-six – Gran's house.

The front door opened even before I had reached the top of the steps. Merlin wriggled, sprang from my arms and wrapped himself round my grandmother's slippered feet.

'Hello, love,' Gran greeted me, smiling. 'Come in. Come in. I've just made us a nice pot of tea, and there's a macaroni cheese bubbling away in the oven. And there's your favourite Neapolitan ice-cream in the freezer for later.'

I kissed Gran on her smooth cheek and let her give me a squeeze. I could smell the sweet toilet water she used and the clean, open-air perfume of her freshly-laundered cotton dress. She was a stickler for cleanliness, was my gran. Always had been. Ever since I can remember there was always a line of washing blowing dry in her neat back garden. And whenever I slept over, which was fairly regularly, the sheets had that lovely smell about them, too.

'Why's Mum late, do you know?' I called after my grandmother as she walked ahead of me to her small, old-fashioned back kitchen.

Gran shook her head. 'Not really, love,' she said, then added, 'but she said it could lead to a promotion, so it's got to be for the better, hasn't it?'

'Has it?' I rejoined unenthusiastically, without thinking.

My gran glanced questioningly over her shoulder as she poured the tea into two cups. 'Well, I should think so, sweet,' she said. 'You know how your mother loves her work.'

I nodded, staring out at the line of pristine washing fluttering in the evening breeze. Oh, I knew how Mum loved her job all right! The trouble was, I wondered if Mum, with her career as a buyer for the local Bentlors department store, and Dad with his travel agency, ever really wanted me. Sometimes, I doubted it. Not that I ever went without anything. On the contrary. If anything, my folks were over-generous. But then, I suppose, with two salaries coming in they could afford to be. No, it was just that our life at home seemed to be run to their job time-tables, and that invariably meant I spent most of my time round at my Gran's house.

'Penny for them?'

I glanced back to Gran who was handing me a cup of tea. I forced a smile and shook my head. 'Not worth a penny, Gran,' I said, taking the tea and thanking her. Merlin started to press himself against my feet, sending shivers up my calves.

'He wants his dinner,' Gran said, bending over and scratching behind Merlin's ear. 'Come on, let's get your dish,' she said, straightening up. She stopped half-way up her hand going to rub her back.

'What's wrong?' I asked, seeing the pained expression creasing Gran's usually jolly face.

Gran grimaced. 'Just old age, love,' she said, forcing herself to stand up and hobble over to the sink to get Merlin's dish.

I jumped down from the stool I'd been perched on

and placed my cup on the table. 'Leave that. Let me do it,' I said. 'You sit down and have your tea.'

Gran continued to rub the small of her back, her large, lined hands making circular motions against her floral print overall. 'It's been bad lately,' she admitted, sitting down at the table. 'I suppose I ought to go and see Doctor Metcalf, but I don't like to bother him, you know. He's so busy with really sick people.'

I forked Merlin's cat food on to his enamel plate and then threw the empty tin into the pedal-bin under the sink. 'You should go,' I said. 'After all, that's what he's there for, isn't he?' I walked to the back door, opened it and placed Merlin's dinner by the step. He jumped over my feet in his eagerness to reach it. I wached him for a moment, his pink tongue darting backwards and forwards, and then I shut the door and walked over to join Gran. 'Tell you what, Gran. Why don't we visit him tonight? I'll walk down with you for company.'

'Well, I don't know . . .' she said, shaking her head, undecided.

'Right, that's settled!' I said. 'I'll go ring for an appointment, then we'll have our meal and have an evening out together, okay?'

Gran laughed good-naturedly. 'I hardly call visiting the doctor an evening out!' she scoffed.

I drained the tea and placed the cup firmly back on the saucer. 'Can you think of anything better to do?' I challenged her, tossing my straight brown hair away from my face and fixing her with a steely gaze.

Gran shrugged. 'Not at this precise moment, I can't,' she replied. 'But give me time –'

12

'No time allowed,' I said, assuming a playful, bossy manner. 'Someone's got to look after you.' I walked towards the front door, where Gran has her telephone, to make an appointment for her. She'd been complaining of aches in her back and hip for some weeks, but had never done anything about it.

'Listen, young lady, I'm supposed to be looking after you, you know,' Gran called through to me. 'After all, I'm nearly sixty – and need I remind you, you're only just sixteen?'

I laughed. 'So?' I called back. 'It's about time I started repaying you for your favours over the years. Right?' Gran didn't reply, but she chuckled, and then I heard her getting the plates and cutlery out ready for our supper.

I looked up Doctor Metcalf's telephone number in Gran's address book and dialled. A clipped, precise voice informed me that the surgery was closed, and would I please ring later.

'No!' I said. 'I want to make an appointment for my grandmother – *now*.'

The woman paused at the other end of the line, obviously taken aback by my unexpected reply. 'But, we don't take appointments until the surgery is open,' she began, agitated.

'That's stupid!' I said. 'By then, it will be too late to come tonight and my Gran needs to see the doctor right away.'

Again the pause at the other end of the phone. 'Oh, then it's urgent, is it?' she asked, her offhand tone softened.

'How do I know?' I exploded. 'I'm not the doctor!'

'There's no need to be insolent, miss,' came the

retort. 'No need at all. Now, just give me the name, and your grandmother can come in at seven-thirty.'

'The name's Mrs Papworth,' I informed her, tightly.

'And the address?' the receptionist asked, super-efficiently.

'Seventy-six, Scudmore Road,' I replied. 'Do you want me to spell that for you?'

There was a snort of indignation. 'That won't be necessary,' she said. 'Goodbye!'

'And goodbye to you!' I dropped the phone back on its hook and walked through to inform Gran of her appointment.

'Oh dear. That late?' Gran said, placing the bubbling aromatic dish of macaroni cheese on to the already-laid table. 'What if your mother arrives while we're out?'

'What of it?' I asked, shortly. 'It will make a change for her, won't it? Let's face it, it's usually the other way round. Perhaps she'd like a taste of being a latchkey Mum for a change.'

I was aware of Gran giving me a puzzled, uncertain look as she spooned the macaroni on to my plate. Whatever she was thinking, she wasn't telling. But I sort of guessed. I think silently she was in agreement with me. In Gran's day, mothers put their children and husbands first – not second, behind a career!

'I'll leave her a note,' Gran said. 'That's what I'll do. Just in case.'

'Please yourself, Gran', I said, concentrating on my food, and then added, '*She* always does!'

Chapter 2

Mum was waiting in Gran's kitchen when we arrived back from the doctor's. She was drinking a coffee, and smoking. I could see, from the three cigarette ends already in the ash tray, that she'd been waiting for some time.

'So there you are,' she said, grinding out her cigarette and standing up to greet us. 'I was getting really worried about you.' She reached over and kissed Gran lightly on both cheeks.

Mum was dressed in her latest, light-wool suit which she wore with a toning cream silk blouse, and coffee-coloured shoes and bag. Her glossy, ash-blonde hair was cut in a long bob and she certainly didn't look her thirty-eight years – more like twenty-eight. Next to her, I felt like the great unscrubbed. And tatty with it! I might have inherited her long legs and slim figure but the rest of me took after Dad. From my angular nose to my mousy, lank hair and greasy skin. Not that Dad still has spots. He grew out of them, so he has tried to reassure me, when he was my age. Well, that was great for him, but mine are obviously quite happy to stay put on my forehead and chin.

Mum leaned over to plant a light kiss on my cheek – one area on my face which was blemish-free. I moved my head, but not before I caught a whiff of the expensive, French perfume she always wears.

'Aren't you going to ask Gran what the doctor said?' I said, pointedly.

As usual, Mum smiled away my snide remark. 'I

was just about to, dear,' she replied, standing back to let Gran sit on the chair she had just vacated. 'But first, how about a nice cup of tea? Or would you like your favourite cup of hot chocolate, Mum?' she asked, walking over to the fridge to get the milk.

'Mmm, that would be nice,' Gran said, being wooed and won by Mum's usual charm.

'The doctor told Gran she has to rest more,' I shot at my mother as I watched her busy herself with pouring milk into the saucepan and then reach up to get the chocolate from the cupboard above the counter area.

Mum turned to glance over at Gran, who was studying the prescription the doctor had written out for her.

'What else did he tell you, Mum?' she asked.

'Oh, nothing much. He said he thought the pain in my back could be from my hip and he wants me to go to the hospital to have X-rays. He thinks it might be arthritis. But I don't think it is. I can't ever recall anyone in the family suffering from arthritis,' she mused. 'Still, he's given me something to ease the pain until I get an appointment. He seemed more concerned about the palpitations I get. I told him,' she said, shaking her head as if to dismiss the possibility that it could be anything else, 'that it's indigestion. Nothing else.'

Mum stopped mixing the chocolate powder and sugar in Gran's cup and turned to face her. 'What palpitations?' she asked, looking worried. 'You never mentioned you had anything like that, mother.'

'Didn't I? I thought I had, dear,' Gran said, unconcerned. 'Not that they give me much trouble. Just catch me short every now and again, they do. Hey! The milk!' she suddenly shouted. Mum spun round just in time to see the milk foam up and spill over on to the stove.

'Oh, dear,' Mum fussed, her usually calm and capable manner ruffled. 'Ronnie, dear, fetch me that damp cloth from the draining-board will you?'

I did as she asked and watched, bemused, as Mum poured what was left of the milk into Gran's cup, then set about to heat up some more milk. When she eventually turned to hand the hot chocolate to Gran, I noticed a large, unsightly stain on her skirt from the spilled milk.

'Made a mess of that, Mum, didn't you?' I said. Then added snidely, 'Perhaps you'd be better leaving anything domestic to Gran or me.'

If I'd thought my remark would goad my mother, I was very much mistaken because she nodded and threw up her hands in mock-surrender. 'I think you're absolutely right, Ronnie,' she admitted. 'The kitchen was never my favourite room, as you well know.'

I bit my bottom lip to stop making a rude reply. If just wasn't worth it! Mum never did profess to be the ideal housewife and mother. On the contrary, she was always the first to admit that she was the most unmaternal woman she knew.

And the sad fact about that was that a) it was true, and b) she just happened to be my mum!

It was only later, back at home, that I remembered to ask Mum about the reason why she'd been delayed at the store.

'Well, I won't know for certain for some time yet,

but there's a possibility I could be offered the Chief Buyer's position for *all* the Bentlor stores,' she confided, her voice edged with excitement.

'Oh, is that all?' I replied, keeping my voice low-key. Then I added, cuttingly, 'Congratulations!' If Mum was aware of my sarcasm she didn't react to it. But then Mum never did.

Chapter 3

I was still drowsing in bed the following Saturday morning when my bedroom door burst open and something landed with a thud on my pillow, just missing my head.

I opened my eyes, startled, and saw a gift-wrapped parcel blocking my vision.

'Wake up, sleepy-head!' Dad's voice called. I blinked the last of my drowsiness from my eyes and sat bolt upright, grabbing the tinsel-wrapped box in both hands.

Dad's bronzed, handsome face smiled down at me. His grey eyes twinkled happily. 'Well, doesn't the old man get even a welcome kiss from his little girl?' he teased. With one fluid movement he stooped and planted a loud, damp kiss on my nose. One hand pulling one of my plaits at the same time.

I twisted away from his grip and made to push

him away with one hand while still holding the gift with my other.

'Stop that!' I squealed. 'And I'm not little any more – and certainly not a girl!' I added indignantly.

Dad's left eyebrow arched, his lips were curved into his crooked smile. 'Don't tell me I've been wrong all these years then?' he said.

'Oh, don't be daft! I mean I'm not a kid any more. If you haven't noticed, I'm sixteen.'

Dad sat on the end of the bed and looked surprised. 'Now when did that happen?' he teased.

'When you were off on one of your endless trips abroad!' I shot at him, half-seriously.

Dad grabbed his stomach as if he'd just been shot. 'Ouch! That was below the belt,' he gasped, and ducked just as my pillow skimmed past his head. Before I could move, he'd lunged over and started to tickle me unmercifully. The present fell from my fingers as I tried to push Dad away, but he'd caught my tinklish spot under my ribs and I started to laugh. My breath caught in my throat so that I began to choke.

'Stop it!' I gasped, as Dad let up for a second. 'I can't breathe!'

Dad sat back and surveyed the wreck he had helped create which had once been my bed. 'Now look at what you've done,' he said. 'You'll have to tidy up this mess before your mother gets back from the store.'

'Don't I always?' I said.

Dad's bright smile dimmed slightly. 'You're a good girl round the house, I'll say that,' he told me.

'How would you know?' I rudely responded. '*You're* never here.'

Dad stood up and scowled, mockingly. Like Mum, he had a charming way of avoiding unpleasant subjects. They really were quite unique at side-stepping issues they didn't wish to discuss. 'Aren't you interested in the present I brought you back from Greece?' he asked, bending to retrieve it from the deep-pile carpet.

I took it from him and slowly untied the golden bow. 'Let me guess, now,' I said, studying the shape and size of the packet. 'It could be another miniature doll to add to my collection?' I glanced up to see if I'd guessed correctly, but Dad shook his head. 'Well, now,' I continued, sliding the ribbon off the box and starting to unstick the pretty gold-patterned paper. 'How about a pair of leather gloves in red, to replace the last ones you bought me from Spain which I lost?' Again I glanced up, but Dad still shook his head. I shrugged, suddenly weary of playing games. It happened every time Dad appeared from one of his overseas business trips and, after sixteen years, the excitement was beginning to wear thin! Silently, I ripped off the last of the paper to reveal an elegant, blue-velvet box. I stared at it, bewildered for a moment. It was unlike anything my father had ever presented me with before.

'Well, clever puss, open it,' Dad encouraged me.

With an intake of breath and trembling fingers I pushed up the lid and peeped inside. Then, with disbelieving eyes, I lifted the lid right back and stared closely at the delicately-worked gold bracelet which lay nestled against the white satin lining. It was the most beautiful present I had ever been given.

'Like it?' Dad asked, leaning forward and taking it from my fingers.

'Like it?' I repeated. 'Oh, Dad, it's fabulous!' I threw my arms round his neck, hugging him close. 'Thank you. Thank you a million, billion times!'

'Hey, come on. Now *I* can't breathe,' he said, untwining my fingers from his neck. 'How about seeing if it fits?'

'Of course it will fit, silly,' I said, holding my wrist out for him to fasten it round.

Dad finished securing the safety clasp and then smiled happily. 'Looks pretty,' he said. 'What do you think?'

I held my wrist out and turned it round, making the fine links of gold glint and sparkle in the morning light. 'It's perfect,' I said, my voice soft with admiration. And then I couldn't help saying, 'You wait until the girls at school see it. Boy! Will they be green with envy!'

I caught Dad giving me an odd look.

'What's up?' I asked.

Dad shook his head. Then said, 'Nothing, pet. But . . . honestly, I don't think it's the type of thing to wear to school, do you?'

'Why not?'

Dad shrugged. 'Well, it's not really, is it? I mean, you don't want to appear ostentatious or be labelled a show-off, do you?'

'Show-off? Me?' I laughed. 'That's very funny, I must say coming from you. What about you with your gold cigarette case and Dupont lighter, and solid gold Seiko watch? Sometimes you look more glittery than a Christmas tree, if you ask me.'

Dad scowled, his grey eyes suddenly cold. 'That's quite enough of that, young lady!' he said. 'I didn't ask for your opinion so let's drop the subject shall we?'

I sat back in my bed and pulled the crumpled covers over my knees, feeling deflated and angry.

Dad's bad temper disappeared just as quickly as it had appeared. 'Come on, cross-patch,' he said, heading for the door and smiling back at me over his shoulder, 'how about making us some toast and scrambled eggs while I unpack? I've been travelling since four this morning and I'm famished!'

I made a great show of pushing off the covers and getting out of bed. 'Okay, if you insist,' I replied, without much enthusiasm.

'I insist!' Dad called, before disappearing on to the landing.

It was nearly eleven by the time we'd eaten the last piece of toast and finished our coffee and Dad had related all the details of his latest trip.

'It sounds fantastic,' I enthused, dreaming about the old city of Athens he'd described in such detail. Of the Parthenon . . . the narrow winding streets with their pavement cafés . . . the strange sounding local food — such as moussaka and dolmades.

'What do vine leaves taste like?' I asked, after Dad had described how dolmades were made.

'A bit like cabbage, I guess,' he explained, 'but you don't taste them as such, it's more the meat and rice

22

filling and the spicy tomato sauce they serve it with that you are aware of.'

I cleared the dirty plates and mugs from the table, then ran hot water into the sink ready to wash up. 'Can you take *me* on your next trip?' I pleaded, half-expecting the usual evasive reply.

'Maybe,' Dad said, and I spun round in amazement.

'What?' I almost exploded.

Dad's grin showed white, even teeth against his bronzed skin. 'Well, don't sound so surprised. There's always the chance that I might be able to get an extra ticket,' he told me, taking a drying-up cloth from the drawer and picking up a wet plate.

I turned back to the washing-up, and swished the hot sudsy water over a mug. 'You're only saying that. You don't really mean it,' I sighed. 'You've always taken Mum with you in the past if you've managed to get a spare seat on a flight and I've usually had to stay with Gran.'

'You don't like staying at your Gran's?' Dad asked, reaching for another plate.

'Of course I do! Gran's the best person in the world – you know that. It's just that . . . well, it would be nice to be like a *real* family, just once.' I washed the last plate and pulled the plug from the sink with more gusto than necessary, making some of the greasy water splash out on to my pyjama top.

'Clumsy!' Dad exclaimed, seeing the spreading damp patch. He flicked the tea-towel playfully at me, and I went to snatch it away from him. Then stopped. He'd done it again! Managed to direct the conversation away from something he didn't wish to discuss

– i.e. being a proper, normal family. I glared at him for a second, wanting to tell him how I felt. To tell him I was fed-up with living in separate compartments in the same house. But what was the use? He wouldn't listen. And if he did, he wouldn't even know what I was getting at.

'So – what's eating you now?' Dad asked, sensing my changed mood.

I shook my head, aware of the tears brimming behind my eyes.

'Something I've said upset you?' my father asked, looking embarrassed.

Again I shook my head. 'Forget it,' I said, 'it's unimportant.'

'Just as you say, sweetheart,' he replied, over-brightly. 'Now. How about going and getting some clothes on and then we'll drive down to meet your mother from the store at lunchtime, shall we?'

In the past, the idea would have made me really happy. But at that precise moment, it did nothing for me at all. Don't ask me why. It just didn't.

As we waited for Mum in the car park behind the store it began to drizzle. I stared out the side window at the Saturday shoppers as they sprouted umbrellas and pulled up their coat collars against the driving rain.

'Bet it's not like this in Greece,' I said, by way of conversation. I was feeling as grey as the weather.

'You're right on that account,' Dad said. He peered through the windscreen, scanning the back entrance for a sign of Mum. The heavy metal doors suddenly swung open and I recognized Mum's burgundy leather boot and trim ankle. The rest of her was being sheltered by a large, black umbrella, held protectively over her by a tall, sandy-haired man.

'Wonder who that is?' I said. 'Looks quite dishy – for an older man.'

Dad gave a short laugh. 'Your mother always did have good taste. Look who she married!'

'Boy – what conceit!' I replied.

'It's only the truth, young lady,' Dad said as he opened the car door, ready to run across to Mum.

I watched the scene through a myriad rivulets of water. Dad looking awkward as the rain trickled down his jacket collar. Mum introducing the other man, smiling her pretty, bright smile. The other man shaking Dad's hand. All so civilized and normal. Except that it wasn't. Normal, I mean. What was normal about seeing your father for the first time in three weeks, then driving to pick up your mother from her place of work? Seeing her with another man. . .

With mounting frustration and anger I glanced back at the other shoppers, milling along the High Street. Mothers with push-chairs; husbands and wives huddled together . . . *that* was normal.

'Hello, sweetheart,' Mum said, clambering into the front passenger seat and leaning back for me to kiss her exquisitely made-up cheek.

'Hello,' I replied, my voice sounding hollow as I ignored her welcome and continued to stare out of the rain-splattered window. Mum turned her head fully to look at me. I pulled a funny face at her.

'Something upset you again?' she asked, glancing from me to my father as if expecting an answer.

I shrugged. 'Nothing in particular,' I said, letting her off the hook.

Mum turned back to face the front and reached for the seat belt. 'Well,' she enthused, as Dad backed the car into a three-point turn to drive out the car park, 'what is the plan for our family outing? I must say it's nice. All of us being together like this,' she explained herself.

'And unique,' I added, under my breath. I didn't expect an answer, and I didn't get one.

Dad edged his way into the busy traffic, away from the direction we would usually take to go home. Before I could ask where we were heading, he explained he was just going to pop into the travel agency to see how things were going.

I sighed loudly. I might have known. Work always came first – family second. And me, last!

'Do you think we'll get to see the film Mum?' I asked, petulantly, waiting for her reasons why we couldn't.

They came. But not from Mum.

'Well, I thought I'd treat your mother to a meal out tonight, Ronnie,' Dad said over his shoulder as he negotiated a double-decker bus. 'That's if you don't mind?'

I bit my bottom lip to stop it trembling and swallowed the lump which had risen in my throat. 'Why should I care?' I replied, making my voice sound bored and uninterested. 'Who wants to see *Raiders of the Lost Ark* anyway?'

'The what?' Dad queried.

'Forget it!' I told him, flatly. And for some stupid

reason felt like crying. But I didn't. After all, what girl in her right mind wants to go out with her silly old parents on a Saturday night when she had a chance of staying in with her Gran? I asked myself.

As if reading my thoughts, Dad said, 'How is your Gran?'

'Not very well,' I told him.

'Oh? What's wrong?' Dad sounded genuinely concerned. He concentrated on turning right, pulling over to the crown of the road. The car behind hooted him and Dad threw up a hand in annoyance. 'Bloody impatient lout!' he seethed.

I turned and glanced backwards. The driver was only young – about eighteen – and very attractive. I smiled at him. For a moment he looked taken aback. Then he stuck his tongue out at me. I sunk back in my seat, feeling my face grow scarlet with humiliation. Who did he think he was anyway? God's gift to women? Mum was telling Dad about Gran's visit to the doctor and sounded, for all the world, as if she'd made her go. If it had been left up to Mum, Gran would still be having aches and pains – and palpitations, whatever they were!

Chapter 4

'Did you get to see the film?' my best friend, Cathy asked, after morning assembly the following Monday.

For some reason, I nodded. 'Yep. It was great,' I lied. Cathy had seen it twice and had really rated it.

'Wasn't it fantastic?' she enthused, grabbing hold of my arm as we walked passed the science lab to Form 4A's study room.

'It was good,' I said, trying to think of a way to change the subject.

Cathy ran her fingers through her mop of cork-screw curls and wrinkled her nose, making her freckles fall into a straight line. 'Good? Oh, come on, Ronnie! You've got to do better than that. It was fantastic! The effects – the scenery. And especially the music. What did you think of the music? Wasn't it fabulous?'

'I guess it was,' I said, feeling my cheeks growing pink from persisting with my pretence. Why had I started it in the first place? But then why did I always do it? Telling fibs, I mean. It was stupid. Why lie about seeing a film? It was crazy. But the trouble was, once I'd lied, I couldn't back out of it. So I just went on fabricating the truth until a small white lie became a whole fairytale of make-believe.

I made my way to my desk at the back of the class and began placing my homework books in the drawer section, under the flip-top lid. Cathy did the same at her desk, to my right. On my left, Mary Riley was chatting to Terry Tanner, our class monitor. Mary's one of the prettiest girls in the school – and she knows it! She's also one of the most popular class members. Not that I see why – apart from the fact that her mother's the school secretary, and I reckon the others gang round her to keep in with the Head – via her mother.

'I saw you with your folks outside Bentlor's on Saturday,' Mary said. 'You certainly have attractive parents, haven't you?' She said it in such a way that I knew what she was getting at. That *I* didn't take after either of them.

'Did you?' I replied, pretending not to be in the least bit interested. Then, for some reason I never will understand, I added, 'Actually, they aren't my real parents, you know, Mary. I'm adopted.'

Mary's mouth dropped open a fraction and her turquoise eyes grew larger than normal. 'Oh, I'm sorry,' she said, looking embarrassed. 'I didn't know. . .'

I shrugged, enjoying the awkwardness my lie had caused her. 'That's all right, how could you know?' I said, feigning unhappiness. 'Very few people do. Please,' I added in a hushed, conspiratorial tone, 'I'd rather you didn't spread it around.' I sat down and glanced across at Cathy – she'd obviously overhead everything because her face was suddenly ashen. She was staring at me in utter disbelief.

'What on earth made you say that to her?' Cathy hissed at me, under her breath.

I felt the blood rush to my cheeks. 'Because it's true,' I found myself saying. Cathy was about to respond but just at that precise moment the door opened and Mr Forsythe, our form master walked in.

'Good morning, Form 4A,' he said in his usual sergeant-major voice.

We stood up and said good morning back, and all the time I could feel Cathy staring across at me. It made my cheeks grow even hotter, as I realized she knew I had lied about being adopted. Well, I thought, so what? Mary Riley wasn't to know and that would give her something to think about for a while!

I stole a glance across the aisle towards Mary, she had her head turned and was whispering to Sheila Parker – otherwise known as Nosey Parker, for obvious reasons since she made everyone else's business her own. And from the way Sheila gasped and shot a glance in my direction, I didn't need twenty guesses to know what she had just been told. Well, that settled it. By lunchtime the whole school would know my secret. Except, I thought, that it wasn't a secret. It was a lie. And why I'd told it was beyond me. But it was too late to take it back, so I just had to brazen it out, somehow.

At mid-morning break, Cathy and I made our way to the railings where we usually stood, watching the senior boys' football team practising on the games field.

The wind was cold but neither of us wore our coats. That was for the lower grades. Once you reached the fourth, no girl would be seen dead with her navy raincoat on, no matter how cold it was. And it was cold. It was freezing!

I pulled my cardigan closer and shivered involuntarily. Cathy hadn't spoken a word to me about what I'd told Mary Riley. And her silence really was getting under my skin. 'Go on,' I said. 'Say it then.'

We'd come to a halt by the railings. I leaned my back against them, one knee bent while my hand dug into my pockets. I stared back at the crowded playground. Mary Riley was holding her usual court by the netball post. She was talking with great animation to several other fourth formers. One or two of them stole furtive glances across towards where Cathy and I were standing, but when they saw me watching them, they pretended to look elsewhere. I returned my gaze to Cathy. She was standing looking past me to the games' field, her small, oval face pinched white by the cold wind. There was a wistful expression in her brown eyes.

The silence between us began to make me feel uncomfortable. 'So tell me what's eating you?' I said, truculently, knowing all the time what it was.

Cathy turned to look at me. 'Why do you do it?' she asked, softly.

I was ready to make a great denial about not knowing what she was going on about, but I couldn't bring myself to continue with the whole silly fabrication so I shrugged and dug my hands further into my cardigan pockets, pushing the wool against my clenched fists so that the garment hung half-way down my thighs.

Cathy stopped scrutinizing my face and turned back to gaze at the distant players kicking the football round the muddy pitch. 'To say that – that you were adopted? I mean that's terrible, Ronnie.'

'What's so terrible about it?' I asked, growing

31

suddenly angry. 'I might as well have been for all my parents bother about me.'

Cathy shook her head. 'That's not true, Ronnie, and you know it. Just because both your parents work—'

'What do you know about how I feel?' I snapped at her. 'Oh, you're all right. You don't go home most nights to an empty house, do you? Have to make your own tea . . . eat alone most of the time!'

Cathy reached out to touch my arm but I shrugged away from her before she could make contact. Tears stung my eyes.

'But you have your Gran,' Cathy ventured. Then added, 'I haven't got a grandmother at all.'

'You don't need one as a substitute mother, do you?' My tears were now running freely down my cheeks. I spun away from Cathy, ashamed to let her see me crying.

'Please don't cry, Ronnie,' she said. 'I'm sorry I brought this up. You're right, I don't know what it's like to be alone so much. But that doesn't mean you have to make up all those fairy stories all the time. The others would like you for what you are, if you'd just let them.'

I rubbed my face with the back of my hand, sniffing away my last tears. 'I don't know what you're talking about,' I said, haughtily. 'What fairy stories? Everything I say is true.'

I turned and made my way towards the girls' cloak-room, to the comparative seclusion of the toilets. At least there I could try and get rid of any trace of my tears before the end-of-break bell rang.

'I'll see you in the art room!' Cathy called after

me. But I didn't reply, or turn round, which was stupid because I had to admit that Cathy wasn't just my best friend, she was my *only* friend.

Chapter 5

When I got home from school that afternoon, I found Dad already in the house, waiting for me. His face was lined with worry. 'What's the matter?' I asked, sensing something terrible had happened. I glanced around the empty house. 'Is it Mum? Has something happened to Mum? Why are you home from the agency?' Panic was making my voice rise higher with every question. A lightning thought shot through my mind that this was, in some way, a retribution for lying about being adopted.

'Calm down, Ronnie, for Heaven's sake! You're as bad as your mother. Panicking without reason.' Dad walked ahead of me to the kitchen where I could see he had been drinking coffee, and smoking.

'Will you please tell me what's happened?' I implored, feeling almost frantic with worry.

Dad pointed for me to sit down at the table. I did, like a zombie, while he plugged in the electric kettle for some fresh coffee. 'It's your Gran,' he stated, his voice thick with emotion. 'She . . . she's had an accident.'

I turned to face him, feeling suddenly icy cold. 'Is

she . . . is she dead?' I asked, the last word sticking in my throat so that it came out all croaky.

'No, thank God, she's not dead,' Dad told me and I noticed his hands were shaking as he made us coffee.

I stared at the cup in front of me, hardly able to make his words register in my brain. Not my Gran? I thought. Not lovely, gentle Gran? 'Is . . . is she going to . . . to die?' I asked, my voice barely above a whisper.

Dad finished pouring the water on the instant coffee then sat down heavily in the chair opposite me. 'No. The doctors think she'll pull through. She was knocked over by a lorry. It seems the driver misjudged her speed as she walked across the zebra crossing. He should have stopped, but he didn't. A witness told the police that Gran suddenly stopped half-way across. I guess it was that bad hip of hers playing up which made her stop walking.' Dad raised his coffee and sipped it, both hands cradling the mug.

I stared at him, not knowing what to say. A picture of Gran pushing her shopping trolley across the busy road sprang into my mind . . . of Gran stopping on the crossing because of her aching hip and back . . . then the lorry crushing down on her. . .

'She is going to get better, isn't she?' I said, looking at Dad for reassurance. 'She *is*, isn't she?'

Dad stopped studying a spot on the table somewhere between us and raised his eyes to meet mine. I could see my own fears and misery reflected in them. 'It's her heart as well, I'm afraid,' Dad said.

'What about her heart?' I remembered the talk of palpitations and suddenly understood there was more wrong with Gran than I had realized.

'The shock of the accident,' Dad continued, replacing his still full mug on the table and reaching for his cigarette packet which lay, with his lighter, on the table. 'It brought on an attack. Luckily she was already in the hospital, otherwise God knows what might have happened. As it is, they've managed to stabilize her condition. But I'm afraid she's going to need her hip pinned. She'll be in hospital for a long time.' Dad lit his cigarette and slumped back in his chair. I had never seen him look so drawn and weary and I began to understand just how much he cared for his mother.

'Can I go and see her?' I asked.

'Not tonight, Ronnie,' Dad informed me. 'She's still unconscious. The doctors recommend that she's not disturbed. She's in intensive care and until her heart is stronger they daren't operate on her hip.' He drew in his breath shakily. 'Poor old lady,' he said and when I looked across at him, I saw, for the first time in my life, that my father's eyes were moist with unshed tears. That proved too much for me and the tears which I had been keeping in check overflowed and spilled on to my cheeks.

Dad held out his arms to me and without stopping to think what I was doing, I ran round the table, into the comfort of his warm embrace and buried my face against his neck. 'Oh, Daddy,' I cried, 'it's not fair. Gran never harmed anyone. . .'

Dad didn't reply, he just held me close and let me cry. And I did. I cried for Gran, and for Mum, and for Dad. But also for me.

I was still sobbing quietly to myself when Mum came

back from the hospital and told us the doctors were pleased with the way Gran was rallying round.

I looked at Mum through my swollen, tear-stained eyes. She was pale and obviously tired. Not at all her usual, elegant self. And somehow, it was comforting.

Chapter 6

Visiting Gran in hospital became a routine. At first, Mum and Dad only allowed me to stay a few minutes, worried that too many visitors might tire her. But after the first week, I was allowed to stay longer. Gran would lie in the starched, clinically clean bed, smiling across at me, her hands resting on top of the sheets like two small birds. She didn't talk much at first, just asked the odd question then listened patiently while I answered. I told her school was just fine and that I was studying hard for my exams the following spring, which wasn't exactly the truth.

'They're very important these days,' Gran told me sternly. 'But then you don't need me to tell you that, do you, dear?'

I shook my head. 'Mum and Dad never stop telling me!'

'But they're right, Ronnie, you know. Now, in my young days it was different, girls weren't expected to do much with their lives.'

I nodded. 'Yes, Gran,' I said, trying to keep the boredom out of my voice. Exams – that's all anyone ever seemed to talk about – both at school and at home. Anyone would think we were sitting them in six days – not in six months!

Gran seemed to enjoy having visitors and after two weeks she'd be looking out for us anxiously wanting to know what we'd all been up to. Mum, Dad and I took it in turns to visit her, so that there'd always be someone to cheer her up. Gran seemed to be making a miraculous recovery, so the doctors told Mum and Dad. They said she would probably always have to take tablets for her heart, but her hip had taken the metal pin perfectly and was mending well. Gran kept us informed on how she was doing with the physiotherapy. She made it sound quite amusing.

'I'm supposed to try swimming in another week or two,' she laughed. 'Heaven's above, I haven't been swimming since—' she stopped, trying to remember, then threw up her hands in despair. 'Do you know, I can't even remember the last time I went swimming!'

'Never mind, Mrs Papworth,' my friend Cathy said. Cathy had asked if she could sometimes visit my Gran with me. Of course I'd said, yes. 'I bet you'll look fantastic in a bikini!'

Gran shook her head and grimaced. 'That is hardly likely, dear!' she exclaimed. 'Still, as long as there are no photographers around, I won't mind.' Somewhere outside the ward, a bell rang indicating the end of visiting time. 'Oh, dear. Time flies so quickly.' Gran looked up at the wall clock. 'I expect Sister will be round to hand out our little wonder pills and then the nurses will bring the drinks trolley with our hot milk, or Horlicks.'

'You sound as if you quite look forward to that,' Cathy observed.

Gran's blue eyes twinkled. She reached across and squeezed Cathy's hand as we stood by her bed. 'To tell you the truth, I do,' she admitted. 'It's a bit like being treated like a child again, and that's quite nice, now and again.'

We both laughed. Gran was getting more and more like her old self. Full of mischief and fun.

'Give my love to everyone,' Gran instructed me as I kissed her goodnight. 'And thank you for coming to see me, Cathy,' she said, leaning forward to let Cathy kiss her, too.

'I've really enjoyed it,' Cathy assured her. 'I always told Ronnie she was lucky to have a Gran – and that's before I ever met you!'

Gran took my hand. 'That was a really nice thing to say, Cathy. But then I'm lucky too to have a lovely granddaughter like Ronnie. She's very special to me. We've always been very close, over the years, haven't we, Ronnie?'

I nodded, remembering the many days and nights I'd spent at Gran's house. The days she'd taken me for outings, while Mum and Dad had been busy working. The holidays we'd spent together . . . yes, Gran and I had a very special relationship. A bond of love.

We said our goodnights, then Cathy and I left the hospital, neither of us saying a word. Both lost in thoughts.

*

'She really is a fantastic old lady,' Cathy said finally, as we were waiting for a bus to take us back to our district.

I nodded, stamping my feet up and down to get them warm. It was getting really cold at nights, now the evenings were drawing in. I leaned out from the queue to see if a bus was coming. It was getting foggy.

'What will happen when she's allowed out of hospital?' Cathy asked, linking her arm through mine to keep warm.

We huddled close together. 'What do you mean?' I asked, puzzled.

Cathy pulled her anorak hood over her head. 'Well, she obviously won't be able to look after herself for quite some time, will she?'

The thought hadn't occurred to me. I stopped stamping my feet and considered what she'd said for a moment. 'I suppose Mum will insist that she comes home to us – for a while, at least,' I said. 'I can't see Gran being able to go back to Scudmore Road until she's really well again. But even then, I don't know . . . I mean, if she's always going to have a bad heart, maybe she shouldn't live on her own.'

Cathy nodded and we fell silent, peering through the darkness for sight of a bus. It was getting foggier by the minute. I suddenly wondered how the weather was in Portugal in mid-November, and whether my father would come back with another suntan. It was the first time he'd gone abroad since Gran's accident and although he'd said he didn't want to go, I didn't really believe him. He always seemed to get itchy feet if he was at home for more than a few weeks, despite what he said to the contrary.

'There's a bus now,' Cathy said, pointing to distant headlights.

'How can you tell?' I asked, peering through the swirling mist.

'Homing instinct,' she replied. 'Also wishful thinking. I'm frozen, and famished.'

'Me too,' I said. Then added, 'It's all right for some.'

'Meaning who?' Cathy glanced at me.

'My father, who else?' I told her, pulling a face. 'No wonder he likes to travel. We must all be mad to live in a country with weather like this.'

'It could be worse,' Cathy offered. 'It could snow.'

I remembered her words the following morning when I drew back the curtains to reveal a mystical, white world.

Chapter 7

'I'll give you a lift to school, Ronnie,' Mum said as she gazed out at the still-falling snow. 'But you'd better hurry because the roads are bound to be bad and I don't want to have to go too fast.'

I snatched the last piece of toast off the kitchen table and tried to fasten my raincoat buttons with my left hand.

'Here, let me do that,' Mum said, noticing the mess I was getting into. 'Honestly, pet, I don't know how you can manage to look such a scrag-bag all the time? I wish you'd take more notice of your appearance.'

'What for?' I asked, pulling away from her. I held the last of the toast between my teeth to free both my hands to do my coat up. When I'd finished I noticed I'd managed to leave a butter stain on the lapel.

'Right. Have you got everything?' Mum asked, pulling on brown leather gloves to match her calf-length boots.

I grabbed my bag from the hall chair and nodded. Then remembered my games stuff. 'I won't be a sec, I've left something in my room,' I shouted, as I ran upstairs, two at a time.

'I'll go and start the car,' Mum called up to me. I heard the front door slam as I frantically grabbed a pair of clean games' shorts and my regulation shirt. My sneakers were still in my school locker but I needed fresh socks. I pulled open the dressing-table drawer where I kept my underwear and pulled out a pair of red woolly ones. Mum hooted the horn impatiently from the driveway.

I turned to leave the room, then I saw the gold bracelet Dad had brought on top of my bedside table. Without thinking, I picked it up and I dropped it into my mac pocket.

'The roads are better than I thought they'd be,' my mother said, peering past the slow-moving wind-screen wipers. Snow had settled on the pavements and on some of the roofs, but the road had already been turned into a grey, slushy mess by early morning traffic. I glanced sideways at Mum. She looked as immaculate as ever in her blue-fox coat, which did wonders for her pale blonde hair and creamy complexion. Automatically, my fingers went to the new crop of pimples which had erupted overnight on my chin.

'Stop that, Ronnie! How many times must I tell you not to touch your spots? It will only make them worse.'

I dropped my hand and clenched both of them between my knees, staring glumly out at the pedestrians. 'Hey, stop!' I shouted. 'There's Cathy, let's give her a lift.' And then I saw who she was walking along with – it was Mary Riley! How could she! 'Don't stop!' I almost shouted at Mum as we came abreast of them. 'Drive on! Drive on!' I pretended to be looking across the street, hoping they wouldn't see me, but the slowing down and then speeding up of the car must have caught Cathy's attention because I was just aware, out of the corner of my eye, of her head turning in our direction.

'Whatever was all that about, Ronnie?' Mum asked crossly. 'You could have made me have an accident. Don't ever do anything as silly as that again. You hear?'

'I'm sorry. It's just that I can't stand the girl Cathy's with. She's a bitch.'

Mum shot me a furious look. 'Don't you ever let me hear you use that word again!' she scolded. 'I won't have you using bad language, do you hear me?'

'I hear you,' I replied, my voice a monotone.

Mum concentrated on slowing down as the traffic lights changed to red. Once we had stopped, she turned to face me. 'I don't know what's got into you lately, Ronnie. Really I don't. You never hear your father or me use foul language to each other, do you?'

'That's probably because you hardly ever talk to each other,' I quipped. 'You're never together long enough to sustain a lengthy conversation.'

The lights changed through green to red and Mum angrily pressed the accelerator. The car screeched noisily ahead of the others. I waited for her reaction to my rude reply but, as usual, she refused to comment on it and instead started talking about Gran. Of how well she was doing; and that the doctors thought she would be well enough to leave the hospital in another ten days to two weeks.

'Will she come to live with us?' I asked.

Mum nodded. 'Naturally dear. She could hardly go back to Scudmore Road – even with the kind, friendly neighbours she has there.'

Mum slowed down the car as we approached the school, coming to a halt outside the impressive wrought-iron gates. 'Well, here you are. You're a bit early, but at least you're warm and dry.'

Before reaching for the door handle, I asked, 'Where will Gran sleep? The spare bedroom will be a bit small for her, won't it?'

Mum nodded. 'That's what I was thinking, too. What we'll probably do is move you into the small room and temporarily turn your room into a sort of bedsitter for your Gran. To allow her some privacy. You won't mind that, will you?'

I shrugged. 'No. Not really. And as you say, it will give Gran a bit of privacy.'

It was only later, as I stood taking my coat off in the cloakroom that it occurred to me that by allowing Gran her privacy, I would be losing mine. Still, I thought, it wouldn't be for long and it's the least I could do after all Gran had done for me.

I was just leaving the cloakroom when Cathy came in, pink-cheeked and damp-nosed. 'Hi, Ronnie!' she said, clapping her mittoned hands together to dislodge some caked snow. 'Didn't I see you getting a lift this morning with your Mum?'

I pushed passed her. 'Probably,' I said, shortly. Then walked out into the corridor and made for the assembly hall, leaving Cathy looking after me, a hurt, surprised expression on her face.

We were nearly at the end of the final hymn when I remembered I'd left my gold bracelet in my raincoat pocket in the clockroom. If I hurried, I could go and get it and be ready for our first PE period without being missed. I edged towards the end of the row, ready to make a dash for the hall door the second the Head had dismissed us. But at the end of the row I saw Cathy and Mary Riley. So what? I thought. I didn't have to talk to either of them did I?

I bent down behind the others and shuffled along hoping none of the prefects would see me. As I straightened up, next to Cathy, she tugged my sleeve to catch my attention.

'What's up with you?' she whispered.

I pulled my sleeve away from her. 'If you don't know, you don't need me to tell you!' I hissed back.

The Head was reading out some notices about the inter-schools' hockey and football fixtures and urging us all to support our teams whenever we could. I glanced towards the raised platform where the teachers sat in their caps and gowns, willing the Head to stop and dismiss us. I was getting more and more worried about the bracelet. Supposing someone had gone in while the school was in Assembly, and stolen it? Thefts did occur like that. That is one of the reasons we were told never to bring valuables to school. I closed my eyes and waited.

'Ronnie, what's wrong?' Cathy's voice was edged with concern.

I shot her a hostile look. 'Nothing! Leave me alone!' I said. Just then the Head's voice boomed out that we could leave the hall and proceed to our classrooms. Without waiting, I pulled open the nearest swing doors and made a mad dash for the girls' cloakroom.

When I dug my hand deep into the pockets, there was no bracelet. For a moment I didn't believe it wasn't there. I held my coat in one hand and stared around the grey stone floor, expecting to see the small heap of gold glinting up at me. There was nothing. Again I searched my coat, examined the pocket-linings to see if there was a tear through which the bracelet could have dropped – but there wasn't. Tears of anger and helplessness filled my eyes. I didn't know what to do. The usual procedure for lost property was to report it missing to the school secretary, Mrs Riley. But that wouldn't bring it back! And what was I going to tell my parents?

If only I hadn't brought it to school, I thought. Why did I have to bring it? Miserably, I walked out of the cloakroom and made my way to the central flight of stairs to the top landing where the Head's office and the staff-room were located. The school secretary's office was next to the headmaster's room. I swallowed hard, then knocked timidly on the heavy wooden door.

'Come in!' called a woman's voice, and I gently pushed open the door and walked into the small, neatly arranged office. It was the first time I had ever had to visit it – and the first time I had met Mary Riley's mother.

'Yes, dear?' A plump, middle-aged woman with greying hair was seated behind a paper-ladened desk, smiling across the room at me.

'I . . . I want to report some lost property,' I said, swallowing hard to stop any more tears from springing to my eyes.

The woman reached in a drawer and took out a large, hard-backed book. 'Well, if you'll just give me the details,' she began, opening the book which appeared to be a sort of register of items reported lost, 'we'll start looking into it. Now,' she drew a line under the last entry and, pen poised, she smiled encouragingly at me to give her the details. 'What is it you've lost?' she asked.

'It . . . it's a gold bracelet,' I told her.

For a moment, Mrs Riley's pen stayed where it was without moving. Then she placed it carefully along the spine of the book and indicated for me to sit down on the chair next to her.

'It was in my raincoat pocket,' I went on to explain, sitting down. 'I . . . I forgot about it during assembly and when I went back, it had gone.'

'Oh, dear. Well, I'm afraid this seems to be rather

46

more serious than the usual items I have to log down, doesn't it?'

I nodded, feeling miserable. 'It was a present from my father,' I said. 'From Greece.'

'I see,' Mrs Riley frowned as if trying to remember something. When she looked up again she said, 'Aren't you Veronica Papworth, Form 4A?' I nodded. 'You're in the same class as my daughter, I believe?'

Again I nodded, wondering why she was asking me these questions. After all, what had it to do with my bracelet?

As if reading my thoughts, she gave a thin smile. 'It's all right, dear. It's just that your mother and I went to school together. You probably didn't know that, did you?'

'No, my mother never talks much about her schooldays,' I replied. I could have added that Mum never talked much about anything to me, mainly because we hardly saw each other. But, of course, I didn't.

Mrs Riley scraped back her chair, then walked across to plug in an electric kettle. She smiled as she saw me watching her. Then said, by way of explanation, 'I expect you'd like a cup of coffee, wouldn't you? I always have one about this time, and as I'll have to make a proper report about the gold bracelet you might as well join me while you're here. Now,' she walked back and reached across her desk for the telephone, 'have you let your form master know where you are?'

I shook my head. 'No, I came straight here.' I was beginning to wish I'd never reported the theft in the first place.

'Well, I'll just ask someone to let him know where you are, and then we'll have a coffee and get down to work, shall we?'

Her warm, kindly maternal manner was making me peculiarly uncomfortable.

An hour later, Mrs Riley read back the report she had written and handed it to me to sign as being correct. Then she glanced over it again and nodded, but her smile faded a little as she told me the police would have to be contacted. Eventually she told me I could go, and that I'd be informed of any developments. I thanked her, and gratefully left the room, wishing like mad that I had never, ever laid eyes on the bracelet!

Chapter 8

'Ronnie! Ronnie! Please wait! I want to talk to you,' Cathy called as I, along with a crowd of other kids, made my way out of the snow-covered playground. The weather had become so bad during the afternoon that we'd been told we could leave school early in case the public transport came to a halt. The wind was whipping the icy snow into my face, stinging my lips and eyes. Although I'd heard Cathy calling me I pretended I hadn't, and just carried on walking along the snow-packed pavement.

'Ronnie!' My name was almost screamed in my

ear, then I felt a pair of hands grab on to my arm.

I stopped. Then turned. 'What is it?' I said, nastily, shaking off Cathy's grip.

Cathy's face was like a water-colour painting. All pink-blotched cheeks and lavender nose. White snow flakes clung to her long lashes and outlined her brows. Her lips were almost blue with cold. 'I want to know why you're not talking to me, okay?' she demanded. 'And what's this about you losing the gold bracelet your father gave you? Is it true?'

Angrily, I started to walk away. So, Mrs Riley must have already told her precious daughter, I thought. Great!

'Why don't you go and ask Mary Riley?' I suggested snidely. Then added, 'After all, you seemed to be having a great conversation with her this morning. You are obviously the greatest of friends.'

Cathy hurried to keep abreast of me. As she's about three inches shorter than I am, it was quite an effort.

'Just because you don't like Mary, doesn't mean *I* can't talk to her, does it?' she demanded.

I stopped so suddenly that Cathy had to walk back a couple of paces to join me. 'Look, you know how Mary feels about me,' I said. 'If you're supposed to be my best friend, how come you have anything to do with *her*?'

Cathy shook her head, her blue lips in a tight line. 'I am your best friend,' she assured me, 'but that doesn't mean I can't be friendly with any of the others.'

'It's not *any* of the others I care about,' I said, using her words. 'It's just *one* other – catty Mary

Riley! Okay?' I turned and started hurrying along the road again.

I heard Cathy catch up with me but I didn't stop or slow my pace. 'You're being very silly, Ronnie,' she told me, breathlessly. 'Mary and many of the others would be more than happy to be friends – if only you'd let them. Have you ever thought that maybe you could be wrong? The way you act?'

We'd come to the crossroads and, as the lights were green, I had to stop. Cathy came to a halt beside me. I looked purposefully straight ahead. What did she mean, 'the way I acted?' I was okay. It was the others who weren't!

'For goodness' sake stop acting like a baby!' Cathy made her point by pushing my back, making me lose balance and slip over the snow-covered kerb, twisting my ankle. A short, sharp stab of pain shot up my leg. I bent over to rub it and glared up at Cathy who stood, looking awkward and worried.

'Thanks a lot!' I said, icily.

'I didn't mean to do it, you know it. It was an accident. Okay?' she retorted.

The lights changed to red and I began to hobble across the slush-filled road, although my ankle didn't really hurt me any more. Once we reached the op-posite side, Cathy stopped. Usually we parted com-pany here anyway as she caught a bus in one direction and mine went in another.

'Ronnie. I just think I ought to tell you that Mary knows you're not adopted,' she blurted out.

Anger flooded through me. 'Oh? And who told her? You?'

'No, I didn't! But thanks for thinking that of me.

You obviously don't think much of our friendship, do you?'

Her uncharacteristic burst of anger threw me.

'Well, how could she possibly know then?' I asked, suddenly subdued.

'It's simple. Her mother and yours were in the same maternity ward. They were old friends. That's how.' Cathy dug her hands into her duffle coat pockets. I stared at her for a second, letting her words sink in.

'Okay, great. So she knows,' I finally replied, over-brightly. 'So what does that make me?'

Cathy sighed, shifting her weight from one foot to the other. 'It's just that . . . well . . . some of the kids are saying that if you could lie about being adopted, maybe you could lie about other things.'

'Oh, yes? Like what, for instance?'

'Like your gold bracelet!' Cathy said, avoiding my belligerent gaze.

I felt myself growing first hot, and then cold. I shivered and pulled my coat closer round my body. Then without saying another word, I turned and walked away from Cathy, towards my bus stop. 'Ronnie!' I heard Cathy call after me, but I didn't turn round. There was no way I was going to let her, or anyone else, see that I was crying.

Chapter 9

I waited and waited for a bus until, finally, I decided I was so cold it would be better to walk. The snow was being blown against me in icy blasts, freezing my cheeks and nose. But at least people couldn't see I was crying. I thought about the things Cathy had told me – that Mary Riley knew I'd lied about being adopted, and I guessed that by now everyone else in the class would know too. I sniffed and wiped my gloved hand over my eyes, feeling the roughness of the wool against my chapped skin. I'm never going back there, I decided. *Never*! How could I face all those sniggering faces? And my gold bracelet *had* been stolen!

The memory of the bracelet brought fresh tears to my eyes. My father had told me not to take it to school – and I had – and lost it! I began to feel shivery. Chilled right through my clothes, and a dull ache had started at the back of my head. By the time I'd reached another bus stop, I'd sneezed three times in a row. And by the time I'd let myself in to our house, my throat felt as if I'd swallowed razor blades, it was so sore.

As usual the house was empty, but at least Mum had remembered and turned the central heating up, so everywhere was nice and warm.

I slammed the front door closed and peeled off my damp clothes, dropping them in an untidy heap on the hall chair. My head was really pounding now and I couldn't stop shivering, I felt so cold. Perhaps a hot bath would make me feel warm, I thought, and walked upstairs to run one. While the bath was filling, I went back down to the kitchen and helped myself to some orange juice from the fridge. I remembered reading in one of my mother's magazines that the vitamin C in oranges was good for colds. The orange juice was so icy that it seemed to make my throat even worse. I grabbed a handful of kitchen paper, blew my nose, then went back up to the bathroom. It was filled with steam and the mirror was completely fogged over. I turned off the hot tap and tested the water. It was boiling. I turned on the cold tap, then decided to add some of Mum's expensive bath oil. By the time I'd undressed and slipped into the sweet-scented, bubble-filled bath, I felt like death.

Good, I thought, as I lay back and let my hair fan out like drifting seaweed around me. The water came right up to my chin. If I was really ill it would mean that I couldn't possibly go to school the next day. Or probably for the rest of the week! I closed my eyes, relaxing in the steaming water, and wondered if I could really spin it out? Being ill, I mean. Because if I could make it last at least ten days, it would be the end of term, and then it would be the Christmas holidays, and I wouldn't have to see any of them. Mary Riley most of all!

'Ronnie?' Mum's voice called up the stairs, waking me from a light sleep. 'I'm up here!' I called through the open bedroom door.

Mum's light footsteps sounded on the stairs and then her head appeared in the doorway, 'What are you doing there?' she asked, surprised to find me in bed. She looked suddenly concerned. 'Aren't you well, pet?'

I shook my head, which now felt like lead. Aching lead. And my nose was so blocked I had to breathe through my mouth – which made my throat worse.

Mum walked across to stand by my side. She looked really worried. 'You look very flushed. Why, your hair's soaked with perspiration!'

I was going to tell her I'd washed it, but didn't. Let her think I was worse than I really was. But the truth was, I felt really ill.

Mum leaned down and placed a cool hand on my forehead. It felt wonderful. Then she placed the back of her hand against my cheek; after a couple of seconds, she shook her head.

'Let me take your temperature,' she said. She disappeared out to the bathroom where the medical items are kept in the bathroom cabinet. When she returned, she was shaking the thermometer up and down. Then she checked to make sure the mercury was at the bottom. 'Open up, dear,' she said and I obediently opened my mouth for her to pop the long cold tube under my tongue.

Mum waited for my temperature to register, sitting on my bed, holding my hand. It was something I couldn't ever remember her doing before. I stared up at the pink-toned ceiling, then over at the darkened window. Anywhere but at my mother because I knew that if I did, for some silly reason, I'd start crying. As it was, I could still feel two large teardrops oozing out of the corner of my eyes, to trickle slowly down my hot cheeks.

'Hey! Why the tears?' Mum asked, puzzled.

I just shrugged. What else could I do, with a thermometer in my mouth? Mum wiped away my tears with one elegant, crimson-tipped finger before checking her watch. Then she removed the thermometer.

'What is it?' I asked, taking the opportunity, while her attention was diverted, to wipe my face with the top of my sheet.

'Nearly a hundred,' she said. Then smiled reassuringly at me. 'You must have caught the 'flu, young lady. Well, a couple of days in bed being kept warm and plenty to drink should soon see you better.'

A couple of days, she'd said! 'My throat's so sore, Mum. I can hardly swallow,' I volunteered, laying it on thick.

Mum nodded. 'Probably your tonsils playing up again. They always do when you're under the weather. I'll make some hot honey and lemon and if that doesn't soothe it, I'll pop down after work tomorrow and get something from the doctor.'

I nodded, thinking vaguely that I'd probably have to be *dying* before Mum let anything interfere with her job. But then I suddenly felt very tired. I dismissed it from my mind. What was the point anyway?

Mum leaned over, smoothed the bed covers and gently stroked my still-damp hair away from my hot face. 'Try to sleep, love,' she said. 'I'll bring you up something light to eat later.'

'I'm not hungry,' I said, turning over on to my tummy and hugging my pillow. All I wanted was sleep.

I heard Mum walk to the door, and then stop. 'Oh, by the way. I meant to tell you. I found your gold bracelet under the passenger seat of the car. You didn't say you'd lost it.'

I opened one eye and squinted out at her. 'I didn't know I had,' I lied. Then added to it by saying it must have dropped off during the weekend. There was no way I was going to tell her I intended to take it to school.

'Well, it's a good job it wasn't lost,' Mum said. 'Your father would have had a fit. You really must try to be more careful. These things cost a lot of money, Ronnie.'

I didn't reply. Just grunted and pulled the covers over my head. But even though I was sleepy I kept thinking of how I was going to face telling the school – and in particular Mrs Riley – that my bracelet hadn't been stolen from the cloakroom after all. Supposing the school had already informed the police? *Don't tell them anything*, a small voice whispered inside my head. *Let them go on thinking it was taken during school hours*. But supposing they found out I still had it? my reason questioned.

The easiest thing was to just forget about it because if I wasn't fit enough to go to school, it didn't matter anyway. It could wait. I turned over and lay on my back. The room was in darkness, the only illumination came from the landing light which shone through the crack in the door. I stared at it, thinking about Cathy – and that made me feel really miserable. She'd been my best friend since our first year together.

Just forget about it! I told myself and closed my eyes. When I opened them again, it was morning.

Chapter 10

The next day we were all but snowed in. Not that I was really interested in anything other than sleeping. Mum took my temperature again and then she telephoned her office to inform them that she wouldn't be able to go in – which was quite something for her! I wondered if she would have done the same if the weather hadn't given her a good excuse?

'Feel like something to eat?' Mum asked, placing a jug of lemon-and-barley water on my bedside table. I shook my head. 'I'll try and get you some lozenges or cough medicine from the chemist. That's if I can get the car out of the garage,' she added, peering out the frosted window at the still-falling snow, and giving a rueful laugh.

She was about to leave the room when she suddenly stopped and walked back to stand beside me. 'I forgot to tell you, pet. The good news is that your gran thinks she'll be allowed to leave the hospital in a week. Isn't that wonderful?'

I smiled. 'Yes,' I said, weakly. My head still ached dully and my throat felt as if it had closed up in the night. I wondered how I was still managing to breathe.

Mum sat on the end of the bed and held my hand. 'How do you feel about letting Gran have this room?' she asked, a frown creasing her forehead. When I just shrugged, she leaned forward and lightly kissed my cheek. A drift of perfume was left behind. 'I knew you wouldn't mind,' she said, interpreting my shrug as an approval. 'But we won't talk about it till you're feeling better. All right?'

Again I shrugged. All I wanted was to go to sleep.

I was just sinking into a wonderful, hazy slumber when I heard the telephone ringing. For a second my half-conscious mind pondered as to who it could be, but I didn't stay awake long enough to find out.

Later, Mum said it had been Cathy.

'Oh, what did she want?' I asked, feeling uncomfortable at the fact that Mum had talked to her. Supposing Cathy had said something about what had happened? About the row I'd had with her? And the reasons I'd had it?

Mum gave me a peculiar look. 'To see how you were, of course,' she told me.

'I don't see why she should bother,' I mumbled, snuggling back down into the warm cocoon of my bedcovers. The sheets were beginning to smell a bit. But it wasn't nasty. Just a sort of sweet-sour body smell because they hadn't been aired for two days.

'She *bothered* because she's your friend,' Mum said. 'And friends should care about each other.'

Ex-friends don't care, I thought. But I didn't tell Mum that. She wouldn't have understood.

By Thursday, after Mum had got some antibiotics from the doctor for my throat, I began to feel a lot better. Not that I let Mum know. I still had to string out my illness until the following Tuesday, when school broke up.

'Fancy getting up for a little while today?' Mum asked, placing a breakfast tray on my bedcovers. The

58

smell of scrambled eggs did something peculiar to my tastebuds because, having hardly eaten anything for three days, I was suddenly starving!

'Why not?' I replied, noticing the butter was oozing through the warm toast. I was into my second mouthful of eggs when I realized Mum was watching me. I glanced across at her, my mouth full of the eggs, a piece of toast hovering in mid-air, ready to be munched on.

Mum began to laugh. 'There's not much wrong with you today, is there?' she observed. But before I could deny it and try to convince her I was still very ill, she'd left my room and headed for the stairs.

I'll have to watch it, if I want to stay off school until the end of term, I thought, and made a mental note only to eat when Mum wasn't around. Which wouldn't be difficult because, after the first two days of playing nursemaid and protective mother hen, Mum had left me to go back to work. Not that I cared really, because I preferred my own company. And in any case, she was coming home at lunchtimes and arranging to leave earlier in the evenings to make sure I wasn't quite dying!

Mum came back from visiting Gran on the following Saturday to tell me that she would be coming out of hospital on the Monday. 'It's a good job your cold's better,' Mum said, pouring herself a glass of mineral water. Mum drinks a lot of mineral water and she's always telling me to do the same. It's supposed to be good for the complexion, so she says. But I never drink it. I hate the bubbles going up my nose. 'Now,' Mum said, perching on the stool at the table opposite to where I was sitting, finishing off a banana-chocolate yoghurt, 'what we'll have to do is organize your room for your Gran. I thought we could put one of the easy-chairs from the sitting-room in there, and fix up the portable colour television from here.'

I put down the spoon I had been using and ran my index finger round the inside of the plastic container to scoop out the last little bit of yoghurt.

Mum reached across and slapped my wrist. 'How many times must I tell you not to do that?' she said, scowling. 'It's a filthy habit!'

I jumped off the stool and went to throw the empty pot in the rubbish bin, under the sink. 'Hey', I said, turning round to face her. 'What's going to happen to Merlin? Will he come and live here, too?'

'Naturally,' Mum said, as if surprised I should have thought otherwise. And that surprised me, because Mum's always professed to hate animals in the house. That's why we've never had one. Apart from a gold-fish I once won at a fair. But it died. I guess goldfish don't really get counted as pets, though.

Mum finished her water, then reached for her handbag which was on the table next to her. After rummaging around in it for a while, she fished out a notepad and her gold Papermate. 'I'd better make a list of everything that's got to be done by Monday,' she said. I watched for a while as her elegant writing began to fill the paper, and then I wandered round to her side of the table to read over her shoulder.

Fetch Merlin from house, I read. This was followed by a list of clothes Gran needed. Plus books, jewellery, bed-linen and towels.

'Haven't we got enough here?' I asked, knowing

that the airing cupboard was crammed with masses of clean linen.

'What?' Mum asked, still adding to the never-ending list.

'Bed-linen and towels,' I said. 'Why does Gran have to have her own brought over?'

Mum pulled a face. 'Don't ask me silly questions, Ronnie. Ask your Gran. It's *her* idea to fetch them. She has a peculiar desire to have her own things around her, and while she's still not herself, I'm not going to argue with her. And,' she said, shooting me a meaningful look, 'nor are you. Okay?'

'Me?' I queried, taken aback. 'Since when do I argue with Gran? I've never argued with her. Not once!'

Mum chewed the end of her pen for a second, absently, nodding in agreement. Still, I could see she was worried about something. 'The trouble is, pet, it's one thing seeing your Gran from time to time – and another thing sharing our lives with her.'

'Meaning?'

Mum chewed on her bottom lip and then shrugged. 'Meaning? Nothing, dear,' she said, dismissively. 'We'll just have to play it as it comes, so to speak.'

'Play *what*?' I asked getting more confused by everything she was saying.

Mum retracted the point of her ballpoint then slipped it back into her bag. Next, she tore off the leaf of paper with her list on it and replaced the pad in her bag, too. 'What I'm trying to explain, Ronnie,' she continued, uncertainly, 'is that we'll all have to make adjustments if we are going to avoid upsets. And by adjustments,' she poured herself another glass of water, 'I mean we'll have to learn to give and take. We've led pretty uncomplicated lives so far. Having Gran here will mean quite a few changes.'

'You can say that again!' I gave a half-laugh. 'For one thing, it will mean I don't have to come home to an empty house every night. Personally, I think it's going to be great having Gran live with us – whatever you think!'

Mum shook her head and sighed. Then standing up she took her glass to the sink. 'Why do you always have to twist things round the wrong way, Ronnie?' she asked, wearily. 'And as for having to come home to an empty house every night – anyone would think you were an isolated case. Believe it or not, there are millions of other kids in the same situation.'

'Really?' I replied, feeling tight with anger and frustration. 'Well, I don't know where all the other kids hang out. But one thing's for certain, they are not in Form 4A at Parkhill Comprehensive!' And saying that, I ran out of the kitchen, up to my room and slammed my door.

I sat on my bed and hugged my knees to my chest, rocking backwards and forwards. I thought of all the times I had wanted the chance to bring someone home to tea – like the others did. Of having a mother who would arrange birthday parties, or special treats for me and my friends. Oh, I had birthday parties all right. Usually a family affair – if Dad was around – of dinner at the local Chinese restaurant. But that only happened at weekends. Weekdays were taboo – because of Mum's job.

I climbed down from my bed and went to stand by the window. Outside the sky was grey with snow clouds. Everything looked bleak and cold. People hurried along the ice-packed pavements like scurrying black ants, heads bent, hands jammed into pockets or clutched frantically on to umbrellas.

I turned back into the warm, glowing comfort of my bedroom, but despite the luxury of the fitted rose carpet and cream bedroom units; of my own small music centre and modern, Scandinavian desk and chair, somehow nothing meant much to me. Others, like Cathy, might think I was lucky to have such a lovely bedroom. And to live in such a beautiful, large house – but they didn't understand anything. How could they, when I didn't understand what was wrong myself? Not really. It's just that I would happily have exchanged everything. Given everything up if I could somehow be popular at school. Have lots of friends – as Mary Riley had. But then, I thought, that's stupid – because I hated Mary Riley, didn't I?

Chapter 11

'What *is* that noise you've got on, Ronnie?' Gran asked peering at me over her knitting.

It was Saturday and as usual I was watching my favourite pop show on the television. 'What?' I asked, feeling a tinge of annoyance at having my viewing interrupted.

'It's just that it's a bit loud, dear. It's giving me a headache.'

I leaned over and turned down the volume a bit.

'Ah, that's better,' Gran said, 'it was going straight through me. I can't understand how you youngsters can call that music. In my days, you had real melodies. Songs you could sing along with.'

I nodded, only half-hearing what she was saying, I was too engrossed in listening to *Marillion*'s latest – and in particular *Fish*! I really rated him. Slowly, I became aware that Gran was talking to me again. 'What was that, Gran?' I asked, over my shoulder.

'I said I'd really fancy a cup of tea, if you felt like popping the kettle on, dear. I'd do it myself,' she added, 'if it weren't for the fact that my hip's playing me up a bit today.'

Inwardly, I sighed. But outwardly I said okay and reluctantly ripped myself away from the telly to go and fill the kettle.

While I waited for it to boil, I glanced up at the kitchen clock. It was nearly seven-thirty. Mum's late coming back from the hairdressers, I thought. Then I thought that she was probably doing some late-night shopping ready for Christmas, and that reminded me that I still had some to do.

The kettle started boiling and I took down a cup and saucer for Gran's tea. It was almost an hourly ritual – tea-making for Gran. I'd never realized she could get through so much in one day!

'Do you fancy some biscuits or a piece of your walnut cake, Gran?' I called through to her.

'The cake would be nice, though I do say so myself,' she called back.

I reached for the cake tin, opened it and lifted out what remained of Gran's homemade walnut slab cake. One of the perks of having Gran live with us was home-baked cakes and pies. She was a fantastic cook and since she moved in our house usually had a new, fabulousy homey sort of smell about it. Hardly a day passed without Gran concocting something delicious with the aid of Mum's electric multi-mixer.

I sliced a thick piece of the gooey walnut cake for Gran, and then decided to have a piece myself. Then putting everything on to a small tray, I walked through to the sitting-room.

'There's a pet,' Gran said, smiling warmly at me.

'It's no trouble,' I replied, handing her her tea, then drawing up one of the nest of tables for her to put her cake plate on.

I sank down on to the floor again, my favourite spot when I was watching television, and popped the last piece of my cake into my mouth. It wasn't until I actually was staring at the screen that I realized I wasn't watching *Topstar* – but a re-run of an old Katherine Hepburn and Humphrey Bogart movie. 'Hey! What's this?' I said, turning to Gran.

Gran was sipping her tea. 'Oh, I hope you don't mind, love?' she said, replacing her cup in the saucer and reaching for some cake. 'I'm afraid that noise really was giving me such a headache and when I tried the other channel, I discovered they were showing '*The African Queen*' again. It's a really wonderful film. You'll love it.'

I stood up. 'I've seen it,' I said. I was going to remind her that we'd both watched it the previous New Year's Eve, at her house, when Mum and Dad had gone out to a dinner-dance. But I didn't bother. Anyway, she was obviously really enjoying it and besides, *Topstar* was all but finished on the other side. 'I think I'll go and do some revision,' I said. Then asked, 'Do you want another tea before I go up?'

'If there's one fresh in the pot, it's a shame to waste it, I always say.' She handed me her empty cup.

I laughed. 'Honestly, Gran! One of these days you'll disappear in a sea of tea, the amount you drink!'

'If I haven't drowned yet, I never shall,' Gran shouted through to me as I took her cup to the kitchen for a refill.

I was just about to carry the fresh tea back to Gran when the doorbell chimed.

'Someone's at the door!' Gran informed me.

'Yeah – I did hear it,' I replied. I was going to add, I wasn't deaf, but kept my mouth shut. I was getting quite good at it really. Not that I'd ever had to have much practice in the past. Before I'd got to the front door to open it, whoever was on the other side, pressed the bell again impatiently. 'Okay! I'm coming!' I called, swinging the door open to reveal my mother, her arms laden with shopping. It was amazing! Most people would have looked at least a bit ruffled after a full day – working in the morning, then going to the hairdresser's, and finally shopping all afternoon. But not Mum. She looked as immaculate as ever.

'Well, darling, don't just stand there, help me to take some of these bags indoors out of the rain,' she admonished. 'And there's some more packages in the boot to bring in, too.'

I took the top bags off the pile she had balancing in her arms, then unhooked another one from her gloved fingers. Ever since Gran had come to live with us our weekly shopping seemed to grow and grow.

'There, that's the last bag,' I said, a little later, plonking Mum's Pierre Cardin initialled holdall on to the already crowded table. I was about to start unpacking things, when the phone began to ring.

'The telephone's ringing!' Gran shouted from where she sat, still watching the television.

I glanced at Mum just in time to see her pull a face, and I could guess why. Gran had a habit of always announcing the obvious! Still, I thought, she means well.

'Will you get it?' Mum asked, busy stocking the fridge with butter and cheese.

'I was just going to.' I replaced a packet of Alpen on the table, and headed for the hall.

'Ronnie? It's Daddy!' My father's voice informed me over a terrible crackling sound. 'I'm at Gatwick. Tell your mother I'm on my way. Okay?'

'How long will you be?' I almost shouted back, wondering if my voice could be heard through what sounded like an underwater exploration soundtrack.

'Can't talk,' Dad cut in. 'I've run out of coins for this machine. I'll be back – oh, in about—' But an explosion of pips cut him off. I listened for a second to see if he would be re-connected but the line went dead, so I replaced the receiver and walked back to the kitchen. But before I reached it Gran called me. 'Who was it, Ronnie?'

I poked my head round the sitting-door. 'Dad,' I told her, 'he's on his way home from the airport.'

'What was that, Ronnie?' Mum called from the kitchen. 'Did I hear you say it was your father?'

'Yes,' I called, then joining her in the kitchen I repeated what I had just told Gran. I seem to do that a lot lately, I thought. Repeat things, I mean. First to one, and then to the other. Boy! I thought. Just wait till Dad gets home and we have to have a three-way recorded message. Life will be fun!

'Did he say how long he'd be?' Mum asked, busying herself by filling the kettle.

'That tea's only just been made in the pot,' I told her. Mum handed me a pack of toilet rolls to take up to the airing cupboard, where we always kept them, then continued to sort through the tinned items she'd bought. 'No, I fancy a coffee,' she said with just a hint of exasperation in her voice. 'A strong black coffee.'

I glanced across at her before heading for the stairs and the airing cupboard, but I didn't comment. Somehow I felt it wasn't the right moment.

'Did I hear someone just put the kettle on?' Gran called out. I didn't answer – and neither did Mum.

Dad arrived an hour later looking, as usual, tanned and healthy. His grey eyes glinted bright in his face and during the three weeks he'd been away, looking for new hotels for his company to contract for the following year, he'd grown a beard. 'Well, ladies,' he said, offering a profile to all three of us in turn, 'what do you think?'

I laughed and tugged it. 'If you paint it white you could be a stand-in for Father Christmas at Mum's store,' I suggested.

'I'm not that fat – or old, thank you!' my father said. He glanced across at where Mum was carefully arranging some new decorations on the Christmas tree by the window. 'Well, darling, how do you like your old man with a beard?' he asked.

Mum stopped fastening a glittery red apple on to a branch and gave Dad an appraisal. 'Very—' she searched for the right word, then laughed as she obviously decided on one, 'very playboyish,' she told him.

'Well, if you ask me, it makes you look downright stupid!' We all turned to look at Gran, ready to laugh with her, except we didn't because she wasn't even smiling. For a moment, the silence in the room was embarrassing. I glanced from Gran to Mum, who looked pale-faced and grim.

Dad looked awkward, standing alone in the centre of the room, still being scrutinized by Gran. 'Well,' he said, digging in his jacket pocket and extracting a packet of duty-free cigarettes, 'you know me, Mother. I'll try anything once.'

'You don't have to remind me!' Gran said, unpleasantly. 'I was the one who always had to get you out of scrapes, remember?'

Mum went back to decorating the tree, she stood very straight and stiff.

'Well,' I said, going up and giving my father a hug,

both arms round his waist, 'I think you look very distinguished and handsome. With or without a beard.'

'Do you?' he replied, absently. He didn't sound particularly interested in what I felt, so I stopped hugging him and made for the kitchen.

'Fancy a tea, Gran?' I asked, knowing her answer.

Gran shot me one of her contagious smiles, her bright blue eyes danced in the firelight. 'That would be nice, Ronnie,' she said, 'at least one member of my family considers me.' She gave me a conspiritorial wink. I winked back. But as I busied myself with making another pot of tea I couldn't quite decide if Gran was being nice to me – or nasty to Mum and Dad. Don't be daft! I told myself. It's your Gran you're talking about. And Gran was always nice.

Mum came out into the kitchen a few minutes later, followed closely by my father.

'Shall I pour you both a cup of tea?' I suggested.

'Not for me, thanks, pet,' Dad said, heading for the fridge. 'I think I'd like something a little stronger than tea at the moment.'

'If you're pouring yourself a whisky,' Mum said, 'make it two. I'll join you.'

I looked from Mum to Dad and was about to mention that Mum hardly ever drank – let alone whisky – when Gran's voice shattered the silence, asking if she could have a couple of ginger biscuits with her tea.

'Here,' Mum said, giving me the biscuit barrel. 'Take them through to her, dear. Oh, and Ronnie?'

'Yes?'

'Be a sweetie and close the door after you, will you?'

'That could be difficult,' I replied.

'Oh! Why?' Mum glared at me.

'Because I'll have both hands full, won't I?' I said, indicating both the cup and saucer and biscuit barrel.

Mum sighed loudly, then raised her eyes to the ceiling.

'Ronnie?' My father had a warning note in his voice.

'Okay. Okay, I'm going,' I said, tucking the biscuit barrel under the arm which balanced Gran's tea, leaving my other hand free to pull the door to. 'But I just think it's odd. All this closing doors bit. We never used to close any door in the house.'

And it was true. We never did. But then, I observed, as I took Gran's tea through to her, we were doing a lot of things that we never used to do, since Gran had come to stay.

Chapter 12

Most of the snow had cleared but the last of it still clung to the sides of the gutters and under hedgerows, its edges frozen solid like miniature icebergs by the zero temperature.

'Make sure you wrap up warm if you're walking down to the shopping precinct,' my mother told me.

'I don't want you catching another cold so soon after your last one.'

It was four days to Christmas and I still hadn't bought a present for Gran, or for my father. 'Is there anything I can bring you?' I called, as I pulled on my bright yellow Wellington boots over my leg warmers.

Mum appeared in the kitchen doorway, wiping her floury hands on a teatowel. She was helping Gran prepare mincepies and the cake. There was a tang of cinnamon and spice in the air and somehow the whole house really smelled of Christmas. It was a warm, homely smell and I loved it.

'Well, I could do with some more gift tags,' Mum replied. 'Oh yes, and some balloons.'

'Balloons?' I repeated. 'We never have balloons!'

Mum laughed. 'I know. I just thought, why not balloons? They always look so pretty. I meant to get some at the store but I didn't have time.'

'Okay, balloons it is!' I said.

'Do you need any money or shall I pay you for them later?' Mum asked.

I unclipped my lizard-skin purse which Dad had brought me home from one of his Spanish trips and took a quick look inside. 'I wouldn't mind it in advance,' I replied. 'Just to be sure I'll have enough.'

Mum nodded and returned to the kitchen. When she reappeared, a second later she was holding a five-pound note.

'That's far too much for what you want!' I exclaimed, but she made me take the money from her outstretched hand.

'Well, you might need the change,' Mum said,

kindly and I leaned forward quickly and gave her a hug.

'Thanks, Mum,' I said. 'You're the best.'

'If you ask me, you give that girl far too much money for her own good,' Gran's voice complained from the direction of the kitchen. It was amazing how she overheard everything anyone said – or did.

Mum smiled and patted my hand, pressing my fingers tightly over the note. I shrugged and chewed my bottom lip, wondering if Gran's comment should be replied to. But Mum must have read my thoughts because she shook her head as if to tell me not to say anything. So I didn't. I just thought it. About how it wasn't really up to Gran to make comments about things like Mum giving me money. Or anything else, for that matter.

'Off you go, pet. And take care,' Mum said. 'And you'd better take an umbrella – just in case it comes on to rain again.'

Mum had walked with me along to the front door. 'It won't rain,' I said, opening the front door and looking up at the dark, menacing, grey sky. I hate carrying umbrellas.

'Don't argue with your mother, Ronnie. Do as she tells you. That's a good girl.' Gran had followed us out into the hall. She stood behind my mother, one arm round a mixing bowl full of butter and sugar which she had been creaming. In her other hand she held a wooden spoon, which was now being waved in my direction.

I glanced from Gran to Mum feeling angry. 'I hate umbrellas, they always get in the way when I'm shopping,' I said, as an excuse.

'And if it rains and you catch a cold, you'll expect everyone else to look after you, won't you?' Gran retorted. 'Well, I can't go running up and down stairs after you — and your mother's too busy with her job — so take the umbrella.'

'No. I won't!' I said, rudely, losing my temper.

The expression on Gran's face set hard. 'Well!' she exploded.

'Mum?' I said, plaintively, looking to her for back-up.

Mum turned back to Gran, and forced a laugh. 'Let her be, Mother,' she said, shooing me out with her hand. 'We really wouldn't ask you to run around after her, you know that.'

'I know one thing,' I heard my Gran say peevishly, as I walked away, 'no child of mine. . .' But I'd already reached the gate and was running along the damp pavement before she'd finished saying just what no child of hers would or wouldn't be allowed to do.

Frankly, I didn't want to hear.

Our local newsagents' was crowded. I pushed my way to the counter and looked for gift tags. Finally, I located them and slipped two packets into my wire shopping basket, then I went looking for Mum's balloons. I discovered them together with a display of streamers and glittery Christmas lanterns. I pondered for a second on what type of packet I should buy. There were so many. The plain round ones; or a mixture of long twisted and round ones; or some which blew up into funny shapes? These were multi-coloured, like rubber sugar candy sticks.

I liked the multi-coloured ones best, but just to

make sure, I selected some plain round ones, too. I was about to make my way to the other counters to see if I could see something for either Gran or Dad when someone trod on my toe, really hard. 'Ouch!' I squealed in pain. I looked up to see whose foot had squashed mine, and found myself looking into a pair of familiar, chocolate-brown eyes.

For a second I couldn't remember why they were familiar. Then I remembered, we had collided previously. At the bus stop when I'd gone to visit Gran before her accident.

The boy must have remembered, too. He shook his head and gave me an apologetic smile. 'Our meetings sure have impact, don't they?' he said. Then added, 'I really am sorry. Are you okay?'

He sounded so concerned that I had to smile to reassure him.

'The last thing I want to do is upset a customer,' he said, smiling a lop-sided, infectious grin.

'It's all right,' I said. 'Really.' I was suddenly embarrassed under his gaze. I tried to edge past him, but he saw my basket, and went to take it from me.

'I could make up for being clumsy by taking your purchases to the pay-in desk,' he offered. And added, 'That's part of my job.' It was then I noticed he was wearing an employee's metal badge on his jacket.

'I haven't finished shopping yet,' I told him.

'Oh, dear. I'm not doing very well today, am I?' The chocolate-brown eyes scanned the other shoppers. 'I only hope the supervisor isn't looking. He'd use any excuse to get me fired.'

'Why?' I asked, surprised at his admission.

The boy hunched his shoulders. 'Ask me another,'

he said. 'Does there have to be a reason these days? Jobs are so thin on the ground you only have to sneeze and they'll be more than happy to replace you. Still, I can't complain. They've been more than fair to me here so far – not like some of the other jobs I've had. Now,' he said, indicating my shopping, 'are you sure a pretty girl like you doesn't want a hand with that?'

I felt my cheeks grow bright scarlet and I lowered my eyes, to concentrate on my yellow boots. 'No. But thanks anyway.'

'My pleasure,' the boy said. 'See you around.'

I watched as he made his way towards the back of the shop. He turned once and gave me his lop-sided grin. It reminded me of my father in a way. And *that* reminded me that I still had to buy him a present.

There was nothing in the newsagents' gift section which caught my fancy for Dad – but I did get a very nice tapestry embroidery set for Gran. It came complete with the stencilled canvas, and the various coloured yarns. I thought it would make a change from her knitting and might give her a new interest. On the way to the pay-in desk I passed the pet food counter and, on impulse, bought a Christmas stocking for Merlin, full of tit-bits and a clockwork mouse. After all, we'd never had a cat stay for Christmas before!

The window of the menswear shop was floodlit and festooned with artificial snowflakes and a large, glittery girl Santa Claus – her sack spilling over to show a selection of present ideas.

I stood gazing down at satin bow ties, cashmere

scarves and assorted silk socks. It was one of the most expensive shops in the precinct and I doubted that I could afford anything. But just in case, I looked at all the tiny price tags. I had just spotted a furry-type hat — sort of Russian style — which was within my budget, when a voice called my name. I glanced up and saw Cathy's reflection beside me in the shop window. For a moment, I froze inside, panicking. Not knowing whether I should speak to her, or turn away. Finally, without turning towards her, I said, 'Hello.'

'Trying to find something for your father?' she asked, and I nodded. 'It's awful, isn't it?' she went on, as if nothing had happened. That we had never had the row before the end of term.

I nodded, then pointed to the hat which had taken my fancy. 'I thought I might buy that,' I said. Then shyly asked, 'What do you think?'

'I think that's a great idea,' she said, enthused. 'Do you want me to come in with you?'

I turned to look at her. She had on a bright pink knitted hat with a large purple pom-pom on top. It made her look like an over-sized pixie. I couldn't help but smile. Automatically, her hand shot to her head. 'What do you think of it?' she asked, brightly. 'Crazy, isn't it? My married sister made it for me but as it's so cold, she said I could wear it before Christmas. Big deal!'

'I think it's fun,' I said.

Cathy peered closer at me through the darkness.

'You taking the mickey? Or are you serious?' she asked.

'I'm serious! Honestly,' I assured her.

77

'Well, if you like, I could ask her to knit one for you – after all you are my best friend.'

We stared at each other for a moment, letting her words sink in. Then she smiled and linked her arm through mine and led me into the brightly-lit shop. 'Well, we are, aren't we?' she said. And I nodded.

'I never did ring back and say thanks for asking about me when I went down with 'flu. It was nice of you to do that,' I said, feeling stupid for being so stupid.

'That's what friends are for,' Cathy said. And it reminded me of what Mum had said at the time – about friends caring about each other – and I knew she was right, because if I had been honest with myself I would have admitted that I'd missed Cathy over the past three weeks. Really missed her.

After I'd bought the hat, Cathy and I decided to have a coffee at the Wimpy bar. We had to wait for a table, but eventually we managed to squeeze in beside an elderly man and his wife.

'What have you got planned for Christmas?' Cathy asked sipping gingerly from her cup.

'Not a lot!' I quipped. 'Gran's living with us now, so I suppose we'll be spending it quietly at home.'

'Me too,' Cathy said. 'We usually have my sister and brother-in-law and the twins over. And my aunt and uncle, and cousin are coming, too. Should be one long, wonderful bore!'

I laughed, and the old lady next to me smiled too.

'What about New Year?' Cathy asked.

I shrugged. 'Don't know. Usually Mum and Dad go to some do – a dinner-dance, or a party at one of their friends. I usually stay over at Gran's.'

'Fancy coming to a party with me this year?' Cathy asked.

I stopped my coffee cup in mid-air, then placed it squarely back in its saucer again with such force, that some of the contents slurped on to the table-top. I glanced up to see if the old couple had noticed, but they were too engrossed in their own conversation.

'A party?' I said, feeling nervous. 'What . . . sort of party?'

Cathy laughed. 'And what sort of parties do you usually go to, silly? It's a New Year's Eve party, of course!'

'Well, I don't know. . .' I began, but Cathy shook her head.

'Go on, be daring, say, yes. You won't regret it. It's a fancy dress affair – you don't *have* to dress up if you don't want to, but it should be fun.'

'Who's party is it?' I asked, the idea beginning to appeal to me.

'My cousin's. It's sort of a combined one really. He's eighteen on Boxing Day and my aunt and uncle have agreed to pay for a disco-party. How about it?'

'Go on! Have some fun!' the old man across from me said, having tuned-in to Cathy's conversation.

'You're only young once!' his wife added. 'Enjoy it! That's my advice.'

Cathy was beaming at them. 'See. You're out-voted – you're coming.'

I finished my coffee. It was cold. But I didn't even notice. I was too excited about the party.

'I'll telephone to give you the details later,' she said, glancing at her watch. 'Crikey! I'll be shot. It's nearly seven and I said I'd be home by six. Mum's waiting to go out and I'm supposed to babysit. Say,' she added, standing up and gathering her shopping bags around her, 'if you're not doing anything to-night, why don't you come over later and help look after my dratted kid brother?'

'I'd love to,' I said, following her out into the darkened street.

'But?' she prompted.

I shrugged. 'I've promised to stay in and keep Gran company,' I explained. 'My folks are going to the cinema.'

Cathy sighed, theatrically. 'Great, isn't it? Me hav-ing to babysit a kid brother – and you your Gran!'

'Oh,' I said quickly, 'I don't mind keeping Gran company.'

Cathy smiled. 'No, she's lovely.' Then she added, 'Give her my love, won't you?'

'Sure,' I agreed. 'And you will ring, won't you?' I said as we parted to go our separate ways. 'About the party?'

'You bet. But I'll ring anyway and maybe we could get together before or during Christmas. What do you think?'

'I think that's great,' I said. And it was. I felt happier and brighter than I'd felt for ages ... even the prospect of staying in with Gran for the evening didn't seem so bad. And then I wondered what I was thinking of? I'd always loved being with Gran – in the past. But recently. . . ? It was probably because of her accident, I thought. That was it. And the worry about her heart. Anyone would be a bit short-tem-pered and grumpy at times, having those worries. The trouble was it wasn't just now and again that

Gran got in a mood, it seemed to be more and more often.

When I arrived home, Mum and Dad were eating hot mince pies and drinking champagne. 'Come and join the celebration,' Dad said, beckoning for me to hurry and join them in the sitting-room. Gran was in her favourite chair by the television, a cup of tea in her hand.

'What's it in aid of?' I asked, catching the happy mood as I walked over to take the glass of bubbling white wine Dad had poured for me. Mum handed me a plate of mince pies and I took one, suddenly realizing I was hungry. 'Well, what do I say cheers to?' I asked, looking round for someone to explain what had been happening.

'It's that promotion I talked to you about, remember? Way back before Gran's accident,' Mum said. 'Well, I received a telephone call today – I've got it! I'm now the Chief Buyer for all the Bentlor Stores throughout the South and Home Counties. Isn't that nice?'

'She's a very clever lady,' Dad said, hugging Mum round her slim waist. 'That's why I married you, isn't it?' He pulled Mum closer and kissed her ear, making her giggle. 'Stop that, Jack,' she told Dad, but I could see she liked it.

I sipped the champagne and wrinkled up my nose as the bubbles hit it. It was worse than Mum's mineral water! 'What exactly will it mean?' I asked. 'Apart from more money?'

'More work, no doubt,' Gran said without looking up. 'In my day, a woman's place was in the home –

and she was happy to stay there looking after her husband's needs and the children.'

Dad laughed good-naturedly. 'But that's just it, Mother,' he said. 'Times change. Haven't you heard of equal opportunities? Women's Lib? It's only right that girls should have the same opportunities as boys to make something of their lives. To contribute to it if they have a natural talent. If you ask me, it's a good thing, too. Far too much talent was tied behind kitchen sinks and lines of nappies.'

Gran's cup rattled in the saucer. 'Fine words, they may be, Jack,' she said, getting unsteadily to her feet. I moved over to help her. Gran smiled at me gratefully. 'But I still think a mother should be around to see her children grow up. I never left you or your brother to fend for yourselves.'

I steadied Gran's elbow as she turned to leave the room, but she pointed for me to pick up her walking-stick which was on the floor by her feet.

'Where are you going, Mother?' Dad asked, obviously affected by her outburst.

Gran turned with the aid of her stick to face him and Mum, who hadn't said a word. 'To get your daughter's supper,' she said archly. 'Everyone seems to have forgotten that she hasn't eaten yet.'

I stared from Mum's stricken face, to Dad's crimson one, and then to Gran as she shuffled from the room.

'I'm really not hungry,' I said, over-brightly. 'Gran! Thank you, but I couldn't eat a thing.' And it was true, because I couldn't. My hunger had vanished completely.

'A growing child needs to have regular meals,'

Gran said as if that was an end to any more discussion on the subject.

I glanced at my parents who stood still, tight-lipped, and silent. And then I heard Gran moving crockery about in the kitchen and for a second I just wanted to scream! Instead, I ran out of the room and up to my bedroom. Except that I went to my old bedroom — which was now converted for Gran. I stared around the re-arranged, pink-walled room which I had grown-up in, and burst into tears. Then I ran out along the landing, and up the narrow flight of stairs to the top bedroom.

Just why I was crying, I couldn't have explained. It's just that everything was such a mess! It seemed, that since Gran had come to live with us, instead of it uniting us as a family, she was driving us apart. And I couldn't stand it because I loved all of them. Mum, Dad and Gran. Especially Gran. And I didn't know how to help. What Gran said was right, but then why had it sounded so wrong?

Merlin came stealing silently into my room and jumped up, his long bushy tail twitching about my ears as I lay sprawled on the bed. I reached out and began to stroke him. His back arched against my hand and he began purring loudly. Downstairs, I could hear voices, and then the television was turned on. I lay back and let Merlin curl up in a tight coil on my tummy. After a while he grew too heavy and carefully, I lifted him off. He eyed me with one dreamy, heavy-lidded eye and then settled back to sleep. Mum would have had a fit if she'd discovered him in my room. But the chances of that were slim at that moment, because I heard her and Dad call out goodnight as they left for the cinema. I didn't bother to reply. I doubt if they would have heard me anyway.

After a while, I went downstairs to join Gran. She was sitting in her usual chair in front of the television. And she was crying, softly. I ran over and knelt beside her, putting my arms round her ample waist. 'Please – don't cry, Gran,' I said, feeling my own tears pricking my eyes. 'Please,' I repeated.

Gran patted my hair and cradled my head on her lap. She smelt of mince pies and lavender all mixed up together. I hugged her closer, remembering those special, homely scents from as far back as I could remember.

'They don't want me here, you know,' she said, her voice half-choked with her tears.

I shook my head furiously and stared up at her through my own tear-bright eyes. 'Of course they do, Gran,' I said, trying to reassure her.

She shook her head, the tears running freely now, down her lined cheeks. 'No, they don't. I know. They don't love me. You're the only one who loves me in this house. I wish I was fit enough to go back home,' she sobbed. 'To my own little home. . .'

'Don't talk like that, Gran,' I said. 'Mum and Dad *do* love you. It's just that . . . well, that . . .' I searched desperately for the right words so that I wouldn't hurt her more. 'Mum's just different, Gran,' I said. There was a silence for a few seconds and then Gran blew her nose. I smiled through my tears at her. 'Just different,' I repeated, thinking I had managed to calm her.

Gran nodded, then reached out and smoothed my damp hair away from my face. 'Yes, dear, she is that,' she agreed, she gave me a watery smile. 'Still,' she said, 'in spite of her putting her career first, you haven't grown up to be such a bad girl, have you?'

I looked at her, puzzled, wondering what she was getting at. But before I had more time to think about it, Gran squeezed my hand. 'Fancy making your poor old Gran a nice cup of tea, pet?'

I jumped to my feet, happy to have an excuse to do something. 'Do you want anything to eat?' I asked. 'Another mince pie, perhaps?'

'Why not?' Gran said. 'After all, strength goes in at the mouth, so the saying goes, and I'll need all the strength I can to get me fit and well again. That's if I ever am,' she ended, forlornly.

'Of course you will be!' I gave her a big hug.

'I do hope so,' Gran said, dabbing her lace-edged hanky to her eyes. 'Then I can go back home. I'm not one for staying where I'm not wanted.'

'Don't say that, Gran!' I said. 'It's not true!'

'Isn't it, love?' she said. 'Well, we'll see. . .'

Chapter 13

The telephone woke me up the following morning. I heard it ringing for a while before I realized no one else was up. Bleary-eyed, I struggled into my fluffy housecoat and ran downstairs to answer it.

'Ronnie?' It was Cathy.

'Hi,' I replied, trying to peer through the early morning gloom at the grandfather clock. 'What time is it?'

There was a pause at the other end of the line. 'It's nearly nine,' Cathy said. 'Don't tell me I've just woken you up?'

'Doesn't matter,' I said, 'I think we've all overslept.' I heard someone moving on the landing above me, and then heard the bathroom door close.

'Shall I ring back? I can if you like,' Cathy suggested.

I sat down on the bottom stair and hugged my knees with my free arm. 'No, I'm awake now. What's the matter?'

'Nothing's the matter as you put it,' she laughed. 'It's just that I'm going to go shopping early and I wondered if you'd like to join me?'

The idea of getting out of the house appealed to me. After last night, I felt I needed escape. 'I'd love to!' I said, jumping up. 'How long can you give me?'

'Just as long as it takes for me to get over to your house,' Cathy said.

'Plus five minutes?' I requested.

'Plus ten if you need them.'

'No, five's enough,' I said.

'So — let's say I'll be there about quarter-to-ten, yes?'

'I'll be ready, waiting,' I told her.

I replaced the phone, then turned to run up to get dressed, just as Dad was coming down.

'Got a date?' he asked.

'Sort of,' I said, squeezing past him.

'Not with a boy?' Dad asked, raising his eyebrows.

I felt my cheeks grow hot.

'No! With Cathy,' I said. And fled up the rest of the stairs.

Ten minutes later, I'd washed, slung on my jeans and sweat shirt and was downstairs gulping some orange juice and eating a cold mince pie.

'If we go on eating those pies at the rate we're going, we won't have any left for our Christmas lunch,' Dad observed, pouring boiling water into three mugs of instant coffee.

'Dad,' I said, between mouthfuls, 'Gran doesn't drink coffee any more. She only has tea.'

'Since when?' Dad asked, surprised.

'Since her heart attack. The doctors said she shouldn't have it as it acts as a stimulant.'

Dad's eyebrows arched. 'Well, you do sound knowledgeable!' He emptied one of the coffees down the sink. 'Is there anything else I should know about your Gran?' He didn't say it nastily, but somehow his words grated.

'Yes, as a matter of fact there is,' I replied, facing him. 'Gran was crying last night after you'd gone out. She said you and Mum didn't want her here. And she said she doesn't want to stay where she isn't wanted.' Just remembering how upset Gran had been, made me feel tearful again.

Dad stopped pouring milk into the mugs and looked at me. 'But that's ridiculous!' he said, lowering his voice. 'Why did she say a thing like that?'

'Maybe because she thinks it's true,' I said, feeling suddenly angry at his surprise.

'What's true?' Mum's voice asked from behind me.

I spun round to face her. She was wearing her hand-embroidered kimono which Dad had brought back for her from Thailand. The rich deep emerald contrasted with her fairness. She looked as if she'd never been to bed.

'Gran thinks she's not wanted here,' I said, accusingly, still angry, but not knowing why.

Mum shook her head, the slightest touch of weariness showed on her face. 'Oh, dear,' was all she said.

The door chimes suddenly rang.

'That's probably Cathy,' I said. 'We're going shopping.'

Mum stepped back to let me pass. 'What time will you be back, dear?' she asked.

I shrugged. 'I don't know,' I said. 'But don't wait for me at lunch – I'll probably have a hamburger somewhere.'

When I opened the door, the milkman stood smiling at me, his account book in his hand. 'Merry Christmas,' he said. I stared at him open-mouthed. 'Something the matter?' he asked staring back at me.

'Sorry – I thought you were my girlfriend,' I said, grinning.

The milkman made a great point of looking himself over. 'Don't tell me I came out in my wife's dress today?' he joked. 'It's so dark when I get up, it's quite possible.'

Just then, Cathy appeared at the gate. I waved to her and then turned back to call Mum. But she was already walking down to the front door, her wallet in her hand.

'Have a nice day, pet!' she said. 'And don't worry. About your Gran, I mean,' she explained, her voice low.

'But I *do* worry, Mum,' I said. 'She seems so unhappy.'

Cathy smiled at Mum and said good morning, and Mum smiled back. 'Both of you go and have a happy time,' she said brightly. 'And here, take this.' She handed me ten pounds. 'I want you to have a nice lunch – a sort of early Christmas present, okay?'

'You shouldn't, Mrs Papworth—' Cathy began.

Mum hushed her protests. 'And who said I shouldn't?' she asked. 'But I would ask you to bring a nice bunch of flowers back for your Gran, Ronnie. If you don't mind. Try and get some yellow chrysanthemums – she always did love them.'

'Okay,' I said. But I wasn't at all convinced that a bunch of yellow chrysanthemums was going to make Gran feel any more loved. Still, they might, I thought.

'So what have you got to buy?' I asked, as Cathy and I sat side-by-side on top of the double-decker bus.

'Not a lot, really. Just something for my dratted kid brother, Greg, and a small gift for my mother for the tree,' she told me.

I gazed out of the dirty window along the High Street and as we passed the newsagents' I remembered the boy with the chocolate-brown eyes and lop-sided grin, and wondered briefly if he still worked there.

'Did you ask your parents about coming to the party with me?' Cathy asked.

I shook my head. 'Not yet,' I told her. Then added, 'It wasn't really possible last night.' But I didn't go on to explain why.

'Come on, let's see if we can get off at the traffic lights,' Cathy said, standing and heading for the stairs. 'I want to look around Marks and Spencer's to see what they've got. I really need a new blouse,' she added.

I followed her down the winding stairs and we managed to jump off at the lights – much against the conductor's advice. In fact, he was furious. As the bus drew away, he shook his fist at us. Cathy blew him a kiss.

'Cathy!' I said, feeling embarrassed. But she just laughed.

I followed Cathy around the counters like a lost sheep. She looked at every possibility for a top to go with the new cords her mother had bought her. Finally, she went back to the first one she'd liked – only it wasn't a blouse. It was a lovely, fluffy angora jumper with full sleeves caught in to narrow cuffs and an abstract flower spray designed on the front in beads. There was a choice of either dusky pink or rich cream.

'Which one do you like best?' Cathy asked.

I looked at the pink one and then at the cream. It was difficult to choose. They were both pretty.

'What colour are your trousers?' I asked.

'Grey,' she told me. 'Sort of sludgy grey.'

'Then I think the pinky one would look best,' I said.

Cathy nodded then picked up one of each. 'What are you doing – taking one of each?' I said.

'Right!' she said. 'Now. Let's pay for these and then go and have something to eat. I don't know about you, but I didn't have any breakfast.'

'I had a mince pie,' I told her.

'You're joking! How could you, first thing in the morning? Ugh!'

I laughed. 'They're lovely at any time of day, the way Gran makes them,' I said. And that reminded me about the flowers, and I made a mental note to get them before I went home.

We walked along to the local McDonalds for lunch – and then had the works! We ordered a Big Mac each, with a large portion of french fries, washed down with strawberry milk shakes and then topped with an apple pie!

'Fancy a coffee now?' I asked, wiping the last flake of pastry off my lips. 'We've still got enough money left.'

Cathy shook her head. 'Thanks. But no thanks.' She leaned back, stretching her legs. 'I'm full,' she told me. 'Let's save the change for a tea, later. Actually, you know your Mum's too generous. You shouldn't let her keep giving you money the way she does.'

'Don't you start!' I said. 'I've enough with Gran going on at her about it. If Mum wants to give me it, why shouldn't she?'

Cathy shrugged, but didn't reply.

I scrunched up the papers from the hamburgers, then stood up, looking for a litter box to post the rubbish.

'Here, let me,' Cathy said. 'I'm nearest.' She took the tray from me and tipped everything into the slot of the rubbish container. Then she stood up. 'Ready to get trampled to death again?' she asked.

I laughed. 'We must be crazy to do this voluntarily.'

'Totally,' she agreed.

We linked arms and headed for the exit. It was a struggle as we tried to get past the crowd coming in, but eventually we made it. Not that the street was any less full. On the contrary, it was packed with last-minute shoppers. But the feeling of excitement was great. Like being part of a huge street party. Or riding a big-dipper. 'You know something?' I shouted at Cathy, trying to make myself heard above the constant rumble of the traffic and the hum of a thousand conversations.

'What?' Cathy called back.

'I'm beginning to feel Christmasy at last. You know what I mean?'

Cathy laughed brightly and nodded. She was obviously caught up in the heady atmosphere, too. It was great!

Chapter 14

There weren't any chrysanthemums — at least, not yellow ones. But I did manage to buy a pot of them. And when I presented them to Gran, she was thrilled.

'Actually, it was Mum's idea,' I explained. 'She wanted you to have them.'

Gran's smile faded slightly as she looked up at Mum who was busy laying the table for our evening meal. 'You remembered they were my favourite flower, Paula, that was sweet of you.'

Mum smiled across at Gran, knives and forks still in her hand. 'I'm glad you like them,' she said, pleasantly, but I couldn't help feeling there was an edge to her voice and I wondered what had been said during the time I'd been out shopping with Cathy.

Gran turned her attention back to me. 'Would you give the plant a drop of water, Ronnie? And then I think I'll have it up in my room. It will add a bit of warmth and colour to the place. I must say, I do miss having my own little garden to attend to.'

I took the flowers from her and glanced across at Mum. She was concentrating on laying the rest of the table and if she'd heard what Gran had said, she didn't seem to have minded. Later, I stood in the centre of my old bedroom and wondered where to place the chrysanthemums, deciding eventually to place them on the bookcase unit by the window so they'd get some light.

As I was about to close the door after me I turned back and glanced round the room. It's a pretty room, I thought. And I couldn't understand why Gran had said it needed the flowers to add warmth and colour. It simply wasn't true.

Christmas Day dawned bright and sunny. I shooed Merlin off my bed, where he usually slept, and drew back the curtains. It was only eight o'clock but I was wide awake. Downstairs, under the prettily-decorated tree were a whole mountain of brightly-wrapped presents – and this year I hadn't a clue what my parents had bought me.

Dad was already in the kitchen when I went downstairs. He was wearing his dressing-gown and slippers – and a paper hat on his head, shaped like a crown. 'Who's been celebrating early?' I asked. 'Don't tell me you were pulling the crackers after I went to bed last night?'

Dad placed a finger against his lips, as if to keep a secret. 'Only one,' he admitted.

'Honestly, Dad, you're worse than a child!'

He nodded happily in agreement. 'Believe me, it's a much better life!' he said. 'Grown-ups have the worst of it – so enjoy yourself while you can!'

I busied myself getting down the mugs for our coffee and the teapot and a cup and saucer for Gran's tea.

'Too late,' Dad said, watching me. 'I've already done the honours. Everyone's had an early-morning drink in bed – by courtesy of the man of the house.'

'Oh, and what about mine? I didn't get one.' I pretended to be upset.

'You, young lady, were fast asleep and I didn't think you'd appreciate my waking you. Even Merlin didn't wake up. Which reminds me, you know you shouldn't let him sleep in your room. Your mother would have a fit if she knew.'

It was my turn to put a finger of secretiveness to my lips. 'Sssh!' I whispered, and Dad laughed.

'Your secret's safe with me,' he said. 'A cat I don't mind, but don't let me find you with a boy in your room.'

'Dad! How could you!' I said, feeling shocked at what he was insinuating. My cheeks burned with embarrassment.

Dad handed me the Alpen and a bowl. 'For heaven's sake, Ronnie, don't look so upset. You are sixteen. I would have thought you'd have a boyfriend or two around by now. I know your mother certainly had.'

'That's different,' I retorted, shortly.

'Oh, why?' Dad queried.

I shook my head, not wanting to continue with the conversation. But Dad wouldn't let it drop.

'Why should it have been different for your mother?' he persisted.

'Because she's beautiful, that's why!' I said.

'Meaning?' Dad asked.

I stopped pouring Alpen into the bowl and stared across at him angrily. 'Oh, come off it, Dad! You know what I mean,' I said, and leaned over my cereal bowl, letting my hair fall forward, a curtain against my father's continuous gaze. The next thing I knew, Dad gently lifted my hair back to reveal my face. I pulled away from him. 'Leave me alone!' I said, feeling silly and cross at the same time.

'Ronnie, has anyone told you you're growing up to be a pretty attractive girl, too?' he asked.

'Don't be daft!' I said, cramming a spoonful of cereal into my mouth before I realized I hadn't added any milk. It tasted like sawdust. I stared round frantically for the milk jug, found it and swamped my plate.

Dad laughed, then gently tugged a handful of my long hair. 'You're a strange child,' he mused. 'But one day soon you'll wake up and discover you *are* beautiful in your own way.'

I snorted. 'What, with spots?' I asked. 'Not to mention a crooked nose!'

'Beauty comes from within, young miss,' Dad said. 'And it takes a boy to make a girl realize she's someone special. You'll see.'

I finished my breakfast in silence, thinking over what Dad had said. I knew Mary Riley went out with boys. And even Cathy had admitted she'd dated a couple of times. But then they were pretty and could talk to boys. I wasn't pretty and I could never think of anything to say. And what was more to the point, I told myself, I'd never even been asked out!

'You could have made an effort and worn something more appropriate for Christmas Day than your jeans,' Gran said, disapprovingly, as she came to join us round the tree at eleven o'clock.

I bit my tongue to stop myself from saying anything – after all, it was Christmas and I wanted it to be really nice. So I smiled and told her I intended to change before lunch – after we'd opened our presents.

Gran grunted.

'Here you are, Ronnie; these are for you,' Mum said handing me all the gifts wrapped in gold paper and decorated with scarlet ribbons.

Mum always made a point of choosing one coloured paper for each member of the family, and she always made them look beautiful with matching ribbons and gift tags.

She selected the red-wrapped gifts for Gran and then passed two blue-covered parcels to my father.

I placed my pile on the sofa next to me, then walked around and handed out my gifts. They weren't half as prettily wrapped as Mum's. In fact, next to hers, they looked almost tatty.

For the next few minutes all that could be heard in the room was paper being torn and sighs of oohs and ahs. Most of them coming from me! I couldn't believe what I'd been given. Apart from new jumpers and jeans, I had pretty frilly underwear and zany pyjamas. But the most precious gift of all was a tiny gold watch with an oval face. It was the same design as the bracelet Dad had given me.

'Like it?' Dad asked.

'Like it?' I breathed holding out my wrist for him to fasten it on for me. 'It's beautiful!'

'I'm so glad you approve,' Dad said. 'So how about a kiss of appreciation for it. Okay?'

I threw my arms round his neck and kissed him. Then I walked over and kissed Mum, too. 'Thank you both,' I said. 'it's the best present I've ever had.'

'You haven't seen mine yet,' Gran cut in, and I felt a blush of embarrassment creep up my neck. 'Here, see if you like this,' she said and handed me a small square box. 'Well don't just stand there gawping at it,' Gran said. 'Open it.'

I felt all eyes on me as, with trembling fingers, I unwrapped the flower-strewn paper and revealed an old-looking velvet-covered box. I found the catch and pressed it. The lid popped open and inside was Gran's beautiful opal ring, set in gold.

'Well? Try it on,' Gran said.

I glanced from the blue and pink firey stone to Gran, and then over to Mum. I didn't know what to say. Not that I didn't love it, I did. I always had – ever since Mum and I had first seen it and decided it would be a lovely gift for Gran, for her birthday, five years ago!

'But, I can't accept this, Gran,' I said, shaking my head. 'It's yours.'

'Mine? What's an old lady like me want with a ring like that? No, I'm much too old to wear finery like that. It's for young people to enjoy. I want you to have it, pet. You deserve it. Now slip it on and let your mother and father see how pretty it looks on you. Mind you,' she added, shaking her head, 'you'll have to stop biting your nails now. You can't wear pretty jewellery with chewed fingernails.'

I gave a short laugh and concentrated on placing the ring on my finger but my hands were shaking and I didn't dare look up at Mum because I knew I had tears in my eyes. I wished I'd never seen the ring in the first place. And in the second place that Gran had kept it! It was a cruel thing for her to do – to give away a present which had been lovingly chosen specially for *her*.

'Hey, look at me!' Dad's voice suddenly broke the silence, and blinking away my unshed tears I glanced up. He was wearing the new furry hat I'd bought him and, arms akimbo, he was pretending to do a Russian Cossack dance.

'Hey! You're quite good at that,' Mum said, laughing brightly and joining arms with him as he spun round and round. I grabbed on to his other arm and started twirling too. Good old Dad, I thought.

By the time we'd stopped my head was spinning and we were all breathless – apart from Gran who was engrossed in the tapestry set I'd bought her.

'What a good idea,' she said, looking through the instruction leaflet. 'And it's got everything included in the pack. I shall enjoy doing this. Ronnie, that was a very sweet thought of yours. Bless you, love.'

Dad managed to keep the atmosphere light and happy for the rest of the day, but I couldn't help feeling that somehow it had all been ruined – because of the opal ring. I half-expected Mum to mention it as she and I were drying up after our turkey and plum-pudding lunch, but she didn't. She was wearing the new, ultra pretty, lace-edged apron I'd bought her, and her cheeks were flushed. She looked really lovely.

'Oh, I nearly forgot!' she said, putting down the plate she had been drying and opening one of the cupboards. 'Here, Cathy asked me to keep this hidden until today. It's for you.'

I took the bulky parcel she handed me and felt its contents. It was squashy and soft and somehow I knew in advance what it was.

I was right. In the centre of some tissue paper I found the cream fluffy angora jumper she'd bought in Marks and Spencer's – together with a gift tag, which read simply. *Happy Xmas to my Best Friend.*

'Now that really *is* pretty,' Mum said, admiring it.

'And it will make a lovely change to see you in something feminine instead of your tee-shirt and faded jeans.'

'But I didn't get her anything,' I said, feeling terrible.

'Well, there's still New Year,' Mum suggested. And that reminded me about the party Cathy had mentioned.

'By the way, Mum,' I said, handing her the last glass to dry. 'Can I go out on New Year's Eve – to a fancy-dress party?'

'Well, I don't know. . .' she said tentatively.

'Don't tell me you want me to sit in with Gran again this year?' I said, reading it in her eyes. 'No. It's not fair! I want to go out and have some fun for once. After all, I'm sixteen!' I threw the rubber gloves I'd just peeled off on to the draining-board and rushed to the door. Gran was standing there. Her face ashen. I didn't need to ask if she'd overheard what I'd said. Her look told me everything.

For a second I just stood rooted to the spot, sensing her feeling of hurt and rejection. And then I ran on past, up to the top of the house, to the seclusion of my room, tears scorching my face.

Chapter 15

I didn't go out much over the rest of the Christmas holidays. Most of the time I stayed in my room. I telephoned Cathy to thank her for her present and to tell her I couldn't go to the party – but I didn't tell her why. That I felt too guilty. . .

Gran never mentioned my outburst once. But then she didn't talk much at all. Just sort of sat round the house working on her tapestry, or quietly watching the television.

Mum went back to work a week later and a week after that, after I'd gone back to school, Dad had to go on a short trip to France. The house seemed to be back to normal. Except there wasn't anything normal about it any more. It was like living in a morgue.

'You're very quiet,' Cathy said, as we wandered around the playground the first week back at school. 'Anything wrong?'

I shook my head. How could I try to explain it all to her? She wouldn't understand. But then, neither did I. I loved Gran before she had come to live with us and it didn't make sense that now I found it more and more difficult to be civil to her – especially as, deep down, I knew I still loved her. Oh, it was all so confusing.

'I was sorry you missed the party,' Cathy said, trying to start up a conversation.

'Me, too,' I replied. We walked on in silence until the bell rang for lessons to commence.

'Ugh! Maths again,' Cathy said. 'I'll never pass my GCE in Maths. I just know it!'

'Nor me,' I said.

'You? Come on Miss Brainbox – you'll pass everything, and you know it. You were born clever.'

Clever? I thought. That's a joke! If I were so clever why couldn't I think out some plan to make everyone happy again? It was really getting me down. I was beginning to hate going home. Between Mum and Dad and Gran I felt as if I were being torn in all directions.

Cathy linked an arm through mine. 'Come on,' she said looking at me thoughtfully, 'you're miles away.'

I laughed shortly, wishing I were.

Later that night, I was trying to do some studying when Mum came up to my room. As I heard her footsteps on the landing outside my door, I shooed Merlin under the bed.

'May I come in?' Mum called, popping her head round the door.

'Why not – it's an open house,' I said, looking from my Chaucer, which I was studying for my English exams.

Mum sat on the chair by the dressing-table, elegant as ever in an oatmeal wool suit and burgundy shoes. 'I have to go on a short training course next week, Ronnie,' she said. Then went on to explain that she would be away from the house for at least four days.

'I hope you don't mind being here with Gran on your own?' she asked.

I didn't look up from my book, although my eyes

weren't taking in any of the words. 'Do I have a choice?' I asked.

There was a silence, then I heard Mum shift her weight in the chair. 'Well, you should say if you have any objections.'

'And if I have?' I asked still not looking at her.

Again there was a pause. 'Say so,' Mum said. I didn't answer. I felt too choked up. She was doing it again. Putting her own life before the family. I heard her get up and walk to the door. She waited a second or two before leaving, then softly closed the door after her.

I waited until I leard her footsteps on the stairs, then I closed my book with such a bang that Merlin shot to the far corner of the room and sat staring at me with wide, apprehensive eyes. For a moment I stared at him staring at me. And then I walked over and pulled down my Adidas bag from the top of my cupboard and began to push some of my clothes into it.

Later, after everyone had gone to bed, I crept into the bathroom and added my toothbrush and towel to the bag. Merlin darted through the shadows beside me as I made my way down the stairs, and then let myself out into the dark, deserted street.

What are you doing? I kept asking myself as I walked along the empty streets. But I didn't really know what I was doing. Only that I had to do it. To walk away from everything. . . *Running away isn't going to be the answer*, I told myself. But the truth was, I just couldn't stay at home any more.

Clouds were scurrying across the full moon, and a cold wind whipped along the street. I shivered, as the first drops of rain washed over my face. I turned right at the end of our road, crossed over the High Street, then automatically turned first left. I was half-way up the hill, known as Fords' Grove, before I realized I was heading for our local municipal park.

By the time I'd reached the perimeter railings, it was raining hard. On the other side of the railings, by the side of the artificial lake, there was a wooden shelter. If I could only get to it, I thought, at least I'd have some protection from the rain.

I threw my bag over the railings and then glanced along the street in both directions to see if anyone was coming. It was deserted. Only the constant, heavy patter of the rain splashing on the asphalt road broke the eerie silence. That, and the distant sound of a train, rattling over damp points.

I reached up and secured my sneakered foot on a cross-section and then hoisted myself up to cock a leg over the topmost section of the railings. Then I pulled myself up, flattening my body along the top of the blunt iron supports, before swinging myself clear. I dropped on to the soft, damp grass on the other side and crouched, listening, in case I had disturbed anyone.

The silence of the empty, rain-splattered park crept in close around me. I found my bag and then, still half-crouching made for the coppice of woods close-by, and its comparative safety.

The shelter was really a reconstructed Alpine cabin, donated by some local philanthropist who obviously found it too big for his own back garden! As a child, I had sat on the steps, licking ice-creams or throwing crumbs to the ducks on the lake. The once well-weathered wood was now splintered and scarred with graffiti and the small windows had been boarded up against vandals.

I sprinted across the small open expanse of ground and leapt up the short flight of wooden stairs to the tiny covered porch, cursing as I misjudged the last one in the darkness and cracked my shin. My breath was coming in short, sharp painful gasps and my ankle hurt. I threw my bag into the darkness at the back of the porch, sat down on the rough wooden floor – and cried.

'Hey! Can't a fellow have one undisturbed night's sleep?' a voice asked from the shadows behind me.

I spun round, my eyes peering through the darkness trying to see who had spoken. 'Who's there? Who are you?' I cried, pushing myself backwards towards the porch steps. It had never crossed my mind for one moment that the hut might be occupied.

'Don't look so petrified. I don't eat people,' the voice said. 'I'm flesh and blood not a ghost!'

I heard the sound of someone moving closer through the darkness and then the next moment a lighter clicked, illuminating a pair of chocolate-brown eyes and a familiar lop-sided grin.

'It's you!' I said, feeling myself physically relax. 'God, you gave me a fright!'

The boy had inched forward so that now he sat next to me and I could see his familiar face illuminated in the watery moonlight.

'The girl with the yellow boots,' he said, brightly. 'Fancy meeting you here.'

I started to laugh, mainly from the wave of relief flooding through me, and nerves, I guess.

'Is it a private joke, or can two share it?' chocolate-eyes asked.

'Be my guest,' I said. And laughed louder. After a second's pause, he joined in, too.

Chapter 16

'Ronnie ... are you awake?' the boy called Ted asked. 'Breakfast is ready.'

I opened my eyes, becoming aware of my aching back and cramped legs. I sat up and rubbed my eyes. 'What time is it?' I asked.

'Seven,' he said. 'Here take this.' He handed me a tin of coke and a handful of biscuits. I took them and began to nibble one, looking around the small, musty-smelling room in the light that was filtering through the cracks in the boarded-up windows and door.

'How do you feel this morning?' he asked, sitting cross-legged opposite me, one hand holding a can of coke while the other was tucked across his chest, under his arm for warmth.

I moved my head from side to side, feeling my neck creak. 'Terrible,' I told him. 'Did you mean what you said last night? That you sleep here all the time?'

The lop-sided grin appeared. 'Yep. It's not that bad really. Better than the car parks, I'll tell you.'

'But why?' I asked, letting my eyes take in the sleeping-bag he'd let me borrow and the ruck-sack stacked in one corner. There were a couple more tattered blankets, an assortment of tinned foods and a small Camping-Gaz cooker.

'I told you last night. I can't afford a room on what I get as a wage. Not that there are any rooms around.'

'But what about sharing a flat?' I asked, taking a drink of coke to ease my dry throat.

Ted scratched his head then ran his fingers through his hair, flattening it. 'You need references ... a month's money in advance, or even more. Life's tough out here, lady,' he said. 'Where have you been hiding?'

I drank some more coke and started to eat another biscuit. Ted had told me the previous night that he'd left his home in the North to find a job in London and when one hadn't materialized he'd gone back to a small terraced house in the mining village where he'd grown up, only to have his mother tell him she didn't want him back again. 'So, you think you've got problems?' he'd said, when I'd told him about the mess at home. 'Believe me, you should count yourself lucky. At least you've got a home to go to – and from all accounts, caring folks.'

Now, in the cold, unkind morning light I thought over what he'd said.

'Go home,' Ted had said. 'Before any more time

goes by. It's always easier at first, after running away. The longer you stay away, the more difficult it becomes. Believe me, I knew enough kids who have found that out to their cost. There comes a time when it is easier to keep on running than it is to go back and say you're sorry.'

'Ted?'

'What is it, Yellow Boots?' he said. He insisted on calling me that even though he knew my name was Ronnie, and I kind of liked it.

I smiled across at him, and he grinned back. 'What would you do?' I asked.

'Do?' he queried, studying his last piece of biscuit.

'Yes. Do. If you were me?'

From outside the cabin we could hear the twittering of birds. I shivered. It was freezing.

Ted laughed at my obvious discomfort. 'Well, one thing's for certain. You weren't cut out to sleep rough.'

I became indignant. 'I could get used to it!' I said. 'Boys aren't automatically tougher than girls.'

'A little feminist, are you?' Ted said, throwing another biscuit across at me. I caught it and bit into it. It was surprising how good they tasted in the cold morning air.

'Maybe I am,' I said. Then added, thoughtfully, because it had only just occurred to me, 'I certainly think there should be more to a girl's life than getting married and having kids.'

'So, from what you told me last night, you agree with what your mother's done?'

'No!' I said. Then changed my mind. 'Well, yes . . . oh, I don't know!'

Ted stood up and shook his legs. 'Well, Miss Yellow Boots', he said, 'much as I'd like to stay and chat longer, I can't. I've a job to do. But take my advice – go home. It's much better – and far more comfortable talking things over indoors than it is in a place like this.' I watched as he gathered a few things together and threw them into his ruck-sack.

'Where do you wash and change?' I asked, realizing there weren't any toilet facilities for him in the cabin.

He laughed and started folding up the blankets he'd been sleeping in. 'Are you telling me I need a bath, is that it?' He grinned over at me.

'No. Don't be crazy. I just mean where do you freshen up?'

'There's a public baths not far from here,' he told me. 'Up the High Street. But for day to day use, I use the cloakroom facilities at work. If I get in early enough no one sees me strip off and have an all-over scrub-down.'

I laughed. 'You seem to have it all sorted out. You make it sound quite desirable, you know.'

Ted's smile disappeared. 'Don't believe it!' he said, sounding bitter. 'Yeh, everything's great until the Parkie comes along and finds you. Or the police move you along.'

I realized I'd upset him. 'I'm sorry. I didn't mean . . . well, to make a joke of it.'

The smile switched on again. 'It's okay. But now I have to go. I hate to say this, pretty girl, but I do hope you're not here when I get back from work tonight. You understand what I mean?'

I nodded, feeling suddenly sad at what he was

telling me. That he didn't want me around. That I should go back home. . .

'Hey! Cheer up,' he said, then in two strides he was by my side and before I knew what he was doing, he'd cupped my chin in his hand and planted a light kiss on my mouth. His lips felt soft and warm.

I stared up at him, my head spinning as he walked back to let himself out through the loose boards in the doorway.

'Don't forget to close the door after you!' he instructed, and laughed.

After Ted had left, I sat for a long time huddled in the sleeping-bag, thinking. It was easy for Ted to say go home — but to what? To the miserable silences and unhappy atmosphere? To no one seeming to care about anyone else? To a father who was never home, and a mum who cared more for strangers than for her own family? No thank you!

I glanced at my watch. It was only eight o'clock. I wondered if either Mum or Gran had discovered that my bed hadn't been slept in? And if they had, what they would think? Or do? I laughed wryly as I thought that there was even a chance that Mum would go off to work without realizing I had left home. Had run away. Great! So much for making an impact on her — if impact was what I was trying to achieve.

What was I trying to prove anyway? I pondered. But my mind blanked out. I just didn't want to think about Mum, or Dad — or my Gran, or home. Anything at all in fact which was pressurizing me before I had run away. Go home? Ted had to be mad! That was the very last thing I intended to do!

I stood up and stretched my numbed legs. Pins and needles shot through them painfully. I shivered, feeling cold and miserable. And scared, too, I guess. But despite all these feelings one thing was certain -- I wasn't going home!

The park café was deserted when I walked in an hour later. The woman behind the bar counter was busily buttering slices of floppy white bread and then sandwiching them together with processed cheese and tomatoes. She didn't even look up when I asked for a coffee and a doughnut. The boiling water in the urn hissed and steamed as she added it to the instant coffee powder in a grubby cup.

'Help yourself to a doughnut,' she instructed, slapping the cup down on an equally dirty-looking saucer. 'Sugar's at the end, by the till.'

I placed the coffee on the laminated tray I had picked up and then reached for a jam doughnut. 'How much?' I asked.

The woman had walked along to the far end of the serving area, to the till. I followed her with my tray.

'That's eighty pence, lovey,' she said.

I extracted a pound I still had left from my pocket money and handed it to her. She rang it up, then handed me back two ten pence coins.

As I took it I realized she was looking at me, a questioning expression on her lined face. 'You're about early, aren't you, lovey?' she asked. Then, before I could reply, she added, 'No school today?'

I felt the colour rush to redden my cold cheeks. 'Er . . . no. . .' I replied, pocketing my change. I glanced round to determine where I would sit.

'I see,' the woman said sounding unconvinced. I smiled a watery smile, aware of the disbelief in her voice. I was still aware of her watching me as I walked away, carrying my tray to the far end of the room. I know it was stupid, but I couldn't help feeling she knew I was lying. Was it obvious that I was on the run? Could she see I hadn't slept at home? But that was crazy, I thought. How could she?

I sat down with my back to the counter and wished I had a comb to untangle my matted hair. I felt dirty and crumpled from sleeping in my clothes. And I still ached from the hours spent on the hard, wooden floor.

I sighed, suddenly feeling terribly isolated and alone. For an awful moment tears threatened to flood my eyes. I bit my trembling lip and picked up the doughnut, then just as quickly placed it back on the plate. I wasn't hungry any more and, besides, the lump in my throat wouldn't allow me to contemplate swallowing even the smallest piece of the sugar-coated cake. In fact, I began to feel decidedly sick.

I picked up the coffee, placing both hands round the cup. It was comfortingly warm. I raised the cup to my cheek and felt its warmth against my icy skin. The pungent, aromatic smell reminded me of home, and a wave of depression flooded through me. Suddenly the doors of the café banged open and, startled, I glanced up. Two jean-clad boys sauntered in. They were red-faced and laughing, rubbing their hands against the cold and nudging each other with their elbows. They stood for a moment, looking round – then saw me.

'Morning, sweetheart!' one of them called over, cheekily. 'Been waiting long, have you?'

The other boy snickered and leered at me. I felt embarrassed, and yet angry. Who did they think they were? I lowered my head, ignoring them and pretended to concentrate on my coffee.

I heard them walk over to the counter, still snickering. It was too much. The moment I heard them giving their orders to the woman behind the counter, I stood up and made a bolt for the door – leaving my untouched coffee and doughnut on the table.

Once I was out in the chill morning air, I glanced about, wondering what to do. A young mother, wrapped up in a bright red anorak, pushed a pram by the pond. A black labrador bounded along behind her. I watched for a moment as she made her way purposefully towards the main exit. It was obvious she was heading somewhere. It slowly dawned on me that I had nowhere to go ... no time limit, and I didn't like the sensation. I had to work out a plan. Decide where I was going ... what I was going to do.

I wandered down to the deserted children's play area. The swings and roundabout were still but a toddler was playing on the slide, his watchful mother standing at the bottom, ready to catch him. I couldn't remember one occasion when Mum had taken me to the park.

I walked across the damp tarmac and sat on the see-saw, my legs splayed either side. The worn, wooden seat struck cold through my jeans.

After a few minutes I got up and walked over to the swings. I was so cold, I began to shiver. I pushed myself off the ground and began to work my legs, making the swing go higher and higher. Overhead, the trees were bare, blackened fingers reaching into the grey, overhung sky. The wind whistled past my cheeks, bringing tears to my eyes. I shut them tight and lost myself in the sensation of movement. It took me back to my childhood . . . to the times Gran and I had come here. Suddenly, all the old memories came hurtling back painfully. All those long days, alone, when Mum and Dad were off leading their own busy lives. Lives which excluded me.

I dragged my feet along the ground and stopped swinging. Tears of loneliness and self-pity washed over my face. I was glad I'd run away. Glad. Yet why did I feel so miserable?

Far off, beyond the municipal tennis courts, where the main road runs parallel to the park, I heard the shrill squeal of a police car's siren. A cold wave of fear washed through me. I listened, my heart pounding. By the time the siren had died into the distant hum of traffic, I was shaking all over. Supposing they were out looking for me? The idea sent a fresh wave of panic flooding through me and I jumped off the swing and began sprinting across the grass – towards the log cabin. To safety.

The cabin was dank and gloomy. I stood still, listening – waiting for the siren again. But all I heard was the muffled sounds of distant traffic and some birds twittering excitedly in the nearby hedgerows. Slowly, I sank down on the pile of blankets.

'Hey, you still here?' Ted asked as he stepped through the improvised doorway, late in the afternoon.

I was slumped in one corner, wrapped in his old blankets, miserable and frozen.

'What do you think?' I asked, morosely. It had been the longest and most lonely day of my life and I was feeling more depressed than I ever thought possible.

Ted walked over and crouched beside me. 'You okay?' he asked, concerned.

I nodded. His words had the effect of forcing the tears I had been trying hard to control all day, to suddenly well up behind my eyes.

'You're not crying, are you?' Ted asked, peering forward to get a closer look at me.

I turned my head away, so that he couldn't see my face. 'No, I'm not!' I retorted, angrily. 'Anyway, leave me alone, will you?' The hot tears splashed over and started to trickle down my cheeks.

'You should go home,' Ted said. 'It would be best for you.'

I shook my head vehemently.

'Your folks will be worried silly,' he said.

'No they won't!' I half-sobbed. 'They don't care.'

'You really believe that?' Ted asked. He sat, cross-legged in front of me. 'You're just talking off the top of your head, right?'

'Wrong! You don't know anything, so lay off!' I wiped my eyes on my sleeve.

'I know what you're doing is wrong,' Ted said, reaching out to take my hands. I snatched them back. He shrugged. 'Okay, so we won't talk about it right now – but you're freezing, and I bet you haven't eaten all day, have you?'

I gulped back fresh tears and shook my head.

'Right, Well, as it's payday, I suggest we go have a really hot curry. How about it?'

I smiled, wishing he wouldn't be so kind. So caring. It didn't make sense. We were all but strangers.

He stood up, then reached down to help me. I let him take my hands and awkwardly I got to my feet. I was so cold and cramped, I seemed to hurt all over.

'I've got some money in my Post Office book,' I told him. 'I can pay you back later.'

He laughed and slipped an arm along my shoulders. 'Forget it, it's my treat,' he told me. 'Now, come on. Dry those tears.'

I hesitated for a moment, wondering if it might be dangerous to go outside. Supposing someone saw me. . . ? Supposing the police were looking for me. . . ?

'It's dark out there now,' Ted said, as if reading my mind. 'And the place I have in mind is hardly the in-place. You'll be okay.' He gave me his lop-sided grin. Again, I wondered why he was being so nice? It was odd, but being in his company somehow made me feel safe.

It was nearly eleven by the time we clambered back into the park after having eaten a Madras curry, with all the trimmings. I felt warmer than I'd felt all day and my fear had subsided so that I'd begun to relax and feel less emotional.

I followed Ted back into the cabin and huddled under the blankets while he lit the Gaz cooker and began to heat up some water in a tin can for coffee. I watched him, wondering at his quiet efficiency. His good humour. He had told me more about his background while we had eaten our way through the spicy meat curry and fluffy white rice and, compared to mine, he had had a really tough time. His mother had been almost an alcoholic and Ted and his brothers and sister had grown up with a succession of 'uncles', none of whom had any time for him or the other children. Money had always been at a premium and although Ted had been good at school, he had accepted that there was no way he would be allowed to stay on after he was sixteen.

Now, as I watched him pouring the water into the mugs, I couldn't help but wonder how he remained so happy ... not at all miserable or bitter.

'Ted?'

'Mmm?' He handed me my mug of steaming coffee, then sat down, beside me. He leaned back against the rough wooden wall, his knees bent. Only the flickering light from the cooker's flames illuminated the hut. It could have been eerie, but with Ted beside me it wasn't. It was somehow comforting.

'Ted, why are you so ... well ... nice to me?' I asked. Then embarrassed at my own question, I added, 'After all, I don't mean anything to you. And besides, I'm sort of gate crashing your pad here.'

He laughed softly. 'It's hardly mine,' he said.

'You know what I mean.'

Ted gazed at me over the rim of the mug as he sipped his coffee. When he'd finished, he simply shrugged, and said 'I don't like seeing kids walk along the wrong path, I guess.'

'I'm not a kid!'

He laughed. 'No?'

'No! I know what I'm doing.'

Ted put down his mug and reached in his jacket pocket for a cigarette. I watched as he lit it, the match momentarily casting a small circle of yellow light around him, highlighting his cheeks, his long lashes and the dark pools of his eyes. 'You may know what you're doing – but you've got the reasons all wrong,' he said, at length. And before I could protest, he said, 'I think you expect too much of your folks. There aren't any rules written anywhere that say a Mum has to stay home and mind the kids, and a Dad has to work a nine-to-five day.'

'I never said there were!' I retorted.

'No? Well, you think about it.' He tapped the ash from his cigarette, sending a spray of glittering sparks about him, to fade instantly in the damp gloom.

We sat in silence as we finished our drinks and he smoked his cigarette. And all the time I thought about what he'd said. . .

'Tired?' Ted asked, eventually, taking my mug from me.

I nodded. I was suddenly desperately tired. The strangeness of the day . . . the fear, and the emotionally draining experience of running away had all had their effect.

'Come on, let's get organized then,' he said. He handed me his sleeping bag and I laid it out in one corner. When I had snuggled down into it, Ted spread a blanket next to me and sat down, pulling two more blankets over him.

'If I promise to behave myself, would you mind me kipping next to you? We'll be warmer,' he explained.

For a moment I felt uncertain, but then my fears disappeared. I smiled back at him. 'Sure,' I said.

He leaned over, turned off the gas ring, and then I heard him settle under the blankets. Felt the warmth of his body, reaching out to mine.

I kept thinking over what he had said, about there being no rules ... about my reasons being wrong ... then, eventually listening to Ted's even breathing, I fell asleep.

Sometime during the night, Ted must have put his arm under my head because when I awoke it was still there. Warm and strong. His breath fanned my cheeks and automatically I snuggled closer to the warmth of his body, under the blankets, and went back to sleep.

When I awoke light was shafting through the boarded-up windows. For a long, relaxing moment I lay with my eyes closed and recalled the wonderful sensation of being in his arns. But it didn't last long, because then the realization of *where* I was came flooding back. I sat up with a start as I remembered the nightmare which had intruded my slumbers. That my running away had made Gran have another but this time fatal heart attack. I knew it was a dream, but the reality of it was still with me. Just supposing ... just supposing it were true?

'You thought any more about going back home, little girl?' Ted asked, eyeing me from across the cabin, where he was opening two cokes.

If anyone else had called me that, I would have been mad — but from him, it sounded different. Special.

I nodded.

He didn't ask me what I had decided, but somehow

119

I guess he knew. All he said was 'Fine' and handed me a tin of drink. I took it, and started to drink. The cold morning light had already placed a barrier between us and it made me sad as I realized that despite our closeness in the night, we were still strangers.

Chapter 17

The hardest thing about running away from home is going back. Having to swallow your pride and retrace your footsteps back along the path to the people you ran away from. And all the time not knowing what they are going to say, or if, as Ted found out, they will want you back.

'Thank God! You're safe,' Mum said, opening the door to me. Gran was behind her, her face as pale and tired as Mum's, and I knew then that what I'd done was thoughtless and irresponsible.

'I'm sorry,' I cried, against Mum's cheek. But she hushed me and stroked my hair and held me close.

'Promise us,' Gran said, her voice thin and full of emotion, 'promise us you'll never give us such a fright again, Ronnie. Promise?'

I turned to hug Gran. 'I promise,' I said, and she gave a tearful smile and walked through to the kitchen. 'I'll just go and make us all a nice cup of tea,' she said, and Mum and I looked at each other and smiled through our tears.

It was only later, that I began to tell Mum about where I'd gone and about meeting up with Ted again.

'And he camps out in the park all the time?' Mum asked, incredulously.

I nodded. I was in my dressing-gown huddled in front of the fire in the sitting-room. I'd had a hot bath and washed my hair and felt clean and fresh. A hundred times better than I'd felt when I'd come back from my night in the park.

'But that's terrible,' Mum said. 'Can't he find somewhere permanent to live? A room somewhere?'

'He can't afford one,' I said. 'It's a vicious circle.' And I explained to Mum what Ted had told me. About his own mother refusing to have him back home; about not being able to get enough money together for advance rent for a bedsit. Mum sat opposite me and shook her head in disbelief.

'It doesn't seem possible in this day and age,' she said. 'I just think it's terrible.'

'Ted's not the only one sleeping rough,' I added. 'He said he'd met lots of others.'

'And you say he's got a job at the newsagent's?'

I nodded.

'Well, you must bring him home for supper. I'd like to meet him. After all, I think I've a lot to thank him for, from what you've said.'

'I'd like to do that,' I said. Then added, 'I'll ask him this Friday, if that's all right?'

Mum smiled across at me as I sat, hugging my knees on the sofa. There was a wistful gentle look on her face. 'I think this boy – Ted, he's become something special to you, hasn't he, Ronnie?'

'Special?' I pondered on her words as I stared at

the tiny flames dancing over the coals. Special? And I remembered Ted's laughing brown eyes and the funny, lop-sided grin which reminded me of Dad; of the way his dark hair flopped on to his forehead. But most of all I remembered the feather-light touch of his lips on mine and I smiled, feeling a warmth spreading through me.

'Yes,' I said, 'he is special, Mum.'

Chapter 18

Ted had left the shed before I could see him again. And when I went to the newsagent's, they told me he'd been made redundant – and no, they didn't have a forwarding address. Just his home address in the North.

'I'm sorry, young lady,' the elderly manager informed me, 'but we are not allowed to give out employee's personal details, even if they no longer work for us.'

I stared at my feet, reluctant to leave the shop without finding a way of contacting Ted. My yellow boots reminded me of his pet name for me, and I smiled, remembering. 'What if I leave a letter with you and *you* send it on for me?' I asked, hopefully. 'I'll even give you a stamp. That way you won't actually be showing me personal information, will you?'

The shop-keeper nodded. 'Well, I don't see any harm in that proposal,' he concluded. 'But it certainly isn't usual.'

I grinned, thinking that nothing about Ted was usual. Still, if there was a chance I could contact him . . . even the slimmest chance. . .

'Will you agree to do it, then?' I asked.

'Just this once,' the man said, then stepped back surprised as I leaned forward and hugged him.

I ran back home and wrote a short note, just thanking Ted and giving him my home address. And I asked him to get in touch. Then I sealed it in a plain envelope and stuck on a stamp. As an afterthought, I wrote across the back, *Please forward if necessary*. Then I ran back to the newsagent's and pushed the letter into the manager's hands.

Two weeks later, the letter was returned. On it someone had scrawled, *Gone away!*

Chapter 19

'Gran's got an invitation to go to Canada, to your Uncle Joe and Aunt Gladys,' my mother told me a few weeks later. 'They even said they'd pay for her fare,' she added.

'And?' I said, concentrating on trying to work out an anagram for a crossword puzzle.

'She wants to go,' Mum said, simply.

I glanced up, surprised. Gran had never wanted to travel to Canada before and she'd been asked hundreds of times. 'Why now?' I asked.

Mum shrugged. 'I think she feels that if she doesn't go now, she never will.'

'Will the doctor let her go? I mean with her bad heart?' I queried.

Mum nodded. 'Just as long as she takes it easy, she could travel the world – or so they told her.'

'What was that?' Gran asked, coming to join us in the garden where we were sitting in the bright spring sunlight.

'I was telling Ronnie about the chance of your visiting Joe and Gladys,' Mum said.

I stood up to let Gran sit in the easy-chair by the garden table.

'Thank you, pet,' she said, lowering herself carefully into the canvas seat.

'Do you want to go?' I asked, sitting on the grass opposite her.

'Oh, I think it might be a little adventure for me,' Gran said, a mischievous light making her eyes twinkle. 'After all, I haven't seen my youngest granddaughter yet and I'd like to see what the latest Papworth looks like.' She turned her attention to me. 'Not that she'll be a patch on you. . .' she said.

'Rubbish, Gran!' I said, 'I'm much too tomboyish – you've always said so.'

'Maybe. Maybe . . .' Gran said. 'But you seem to have grown out of that.' She closed her eyes against the watery sunlight and leaned back in her chair.

After a few seconds her breathing became even and she began to snore gently.

I looked over to Mum and we smiled at each other. Then we went back to what we had been doing. Me to my crossword and Mum to her book.

Chapter 20

'Seeing you wearing that bracelet reminds me,' Mum said.

'What of?' I asked stuffing my revision books into my school bag.

'Some time before Christmas, when you had the 'flu – the school wrote to say they were sorry they had no trace of your bracelet. Did you tell them you thought you'd lost it there?'

'Oh, yes, so I did,' I said, remembering. 'What did you say?'

'I just wrote back and said I was sorry they were troubled but we found the bracelet in my car. I had a lovely little note back from Mrs Riley – you know she and I used to go to school together, years ago? Anyway, she said she was pleased we'd found it and that she thought I had a very lovely daughter.'

'What?' I zippered my bag and laughed.

Mum checked that everything was turned off in the house and followed me to the front door. 'What's so funny about that?' she said, shooing me out before her. 'She was absolutely right. You are lovely.' Then she qualified it by adding, 'Sometimes.'

The postman met us at our gate and handed Mum some letters. She placed her handbag under her arm and sorted through them.

'One from your father,' she said, examining a post-mark from Spain. 'And a card from Canada from your Gran – and bills!'

I followed her to the car already parked by the kerb. 'Going to give me a lift on the last day of my GCE's?' I asked.

Mum sighed. 'All right. Get in,' she instructed, then walked round to the driver's door.

As we drew to a halt outside the school gates, I asked Mum when Gran was coming back.

'Oh, not for another month at least,' she said.

'And then what?' I asked.

Mum shrugged and pulled a face. 'I really don't know, pet,' she said. 'She says she wants to try living back in her own house. I think she'd be happier there, but we'll just have to wait and see.'

I opened the passenger door and started to climb out.

'Hey – wait a sec, young lady,' Mum called. I turned to see what she wanted. She was holding out her hand.

'What's that for?' I asked, puzzled.

'You'd better give me the bracelet,' she said, matter-of-factly. 'You know the school rules.'

'Mum!' I exclaimed.

'Never mind the pouting lip – hand it over,' she said.

I unclipped it and let it drop, in a glinting golden heap in her outstretched palm. Her elegant, pink-tipped fingers closed over it. 'There'll be plenty of time to wear all your finery when you go on to college,' she said.

'And who says I'm going on to college?' I asked, climbing out of the car.

'Well, aren't you?' Mum asked.

'Maybe,' I replied, then slammed the door.

I stood watching the car draw out into the traffic, then turned to walk into school.

'Hey! Ronnie – wait for me!' Cathy called running along the road towards me, the sun dancing off her curls.

I waited until she'd caught me up and then we walked through the gates and into the playground.

'Good luck, you two!' a voice called.

I glanced across to see who is was. Mary Riley was waving at us. I waved back.

'Same to you!' Cathy replied.

'Think of it,' Cathy said as we leaned against the railings waiting for the school bell to ring. 'After today – we're free!'

I laughed. 'Yes – but for how long?'

'Who cares,' my best friend replied. And I nodded in agreement. Who cared?

Chapter 21

I saw him again today. The boy with the chocolate-brown eyes and lop-sided grin.

I was on the bus going to Marks and Spencer's and it had stopped by the traffic lights – and there he was, walking along the High Street. I waved frantically, but he was looking straight ahead – not at the bus. By the time I'd fought my way through to the platform, the lights had changed and I'd been carried on to the next stop. And Ted had been swallowed up in the Saturday shoppers.

But I didn't mind. I knew that sooner or later we'd meet, now that he's back in the district. If not today – then tomorrow . . . or the day after.

'Where are you off to?' Mum asked as I'd changed into my new shorts and sleeveless tee-shirt.

'I just thought I'd go for a walk up to the park,' I'd told her. What I hadn't told her was that I was going to the old cabin, to wait. . .

And that's what I'm doing, right now. . .